Praise

Praise for *The Misadventures of Don Kee Dong & Phillip Mihol*

"An over-the-top gay... sendup of the secret-agent genre... with an absurd premise, pulpy fight scenes, and a few serious messages."
— *Kirkus Reviews*

"Magnificent and very funny... Carter breathes life into wild plots and tongue-in-cheek subjects."
— *Matt Sizemore, performer*

"I couldn't stop turning the pages... vivid and wildly entertaining."
— *Dean Phoenix, performer*

"Sophisticated, slutty, and full of surprises."
— *Jesse Zeppelin, performer*

The Misadventures of Don Kee Dong & Phillip Mihol

International Men of Mystery

The Misadventures of Don Kee Dong & Phillip Mihol

International Men of Mystery

GARETH CARTER

LA Notable Books

The Library of Congress

Published by LA Notable Books.

ISBN Print: 978-1-970702-00-2
ISBN eBook: 978-1-970702-01-9

Subjects: LCSH: 1. Gay men—Fiction 2. Spy—Fiction. 3. Satire—Fiction. 4. Secret societies—Fiction. | LCGFT: Novels.

Cover design by Alan Smythe.

Content Notice

This book contains explicit sexual content, including scenes of graphic gay sex and one instance of non-consensual penetration. It is intended for mature audiences only.

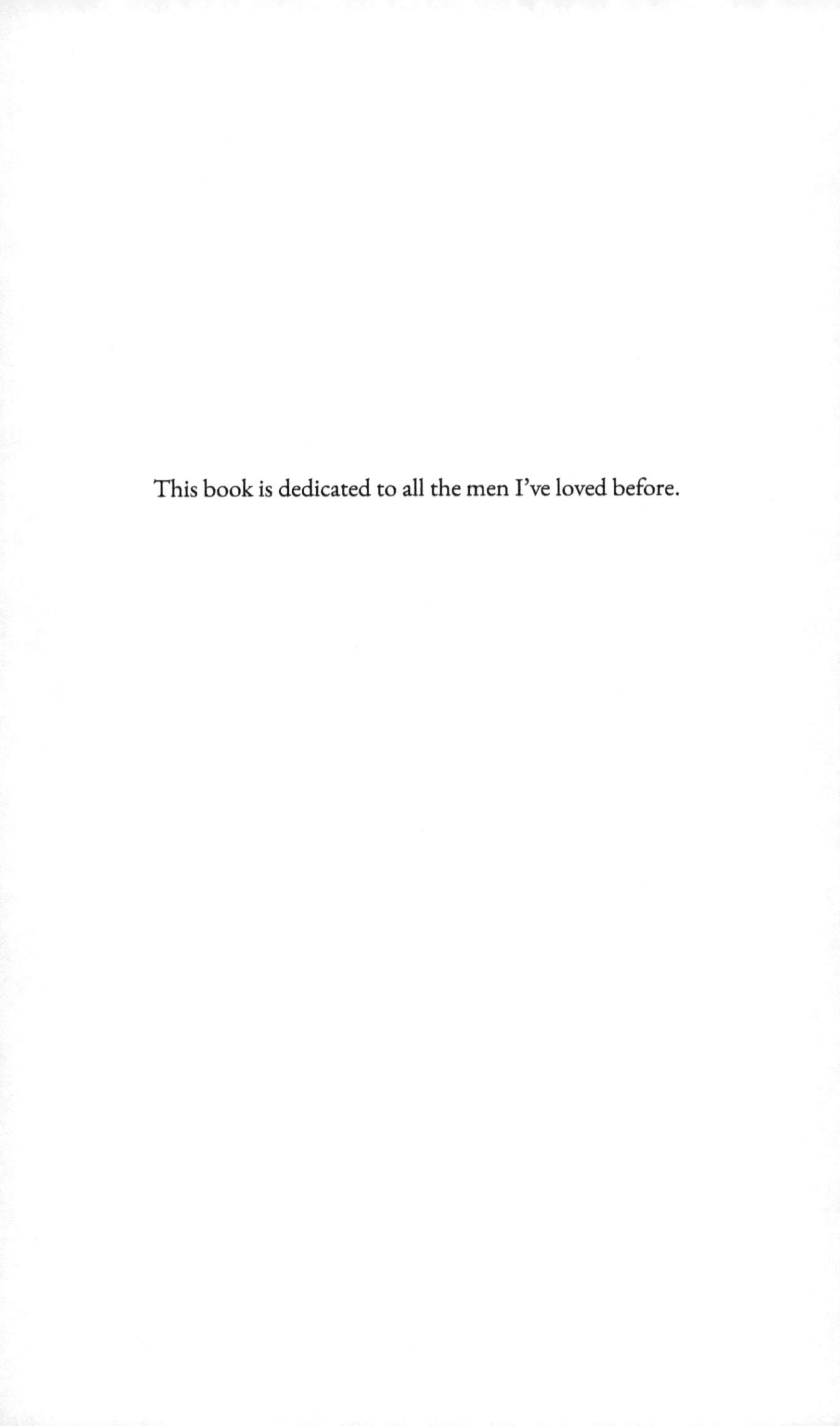

This book is dedicated to all the men I've loved before.

Author's Note

This series was born when I, a mild-mannered librarian, was labeled a "pornographer" for simply making inclusive books available to young readers.

If that's the accusation, I thought, I might as well earn it.

The Misadventures of Don Kee Dong & Phillip Mihol is part spy adventure, part queer travelogue—an irreverent, globetrotting romp inspired by the pulp fiction of the 1960s and '70s. Think James Bond meets *Queer as Folk*, with far fewer rules and far more fun.

I hope you enjoy the ride.

— Gareth Carter

UNITED NATIONS REPORT

This account was discovered buried deep within a decommissioned UN hard drive—like a Russian nesting doll—hidden inside layers of encrypted folders.

Though the device had been marked for disposal, it was never properly wiped. After extensive recovery and decryption, its contents are now being revealed for the first time. – GC

Chapter 1

I awoke to complete darkness, my head throbbing. It was hard to breathe. I surmised from the dusty smell that I had a burlap sack over my head, cinched at the neck. My arms and legs were immobilized, strapped to a very uncomfortable chair. Somewhere beneath the fear, anger simmered. How did I end up here?

"He's awake," I heard a man say.

"He'll be groggy," another said in a thick French accent.

A sharp slap to my head, I tasted blood—fortunately my own. I didn't react.

"Horace Huang?" a man with a Spanish accent said.

I breathed a sigh of relief. That wasn't my real name.

"Or do you prefer, Don Kee Dong?" he then added. "Interesting, one of my very important guests this evening shares your last name. I guess it is fairly common where you all come from. It rolls off the tongue quite nicely."

How did they know my real name? I just grumbled in acceptance. There was no need to fight the truth.

"Señor Dong, I will ask you this once and once only," said the Spainard's voice. "What brings you to Budapest? Do not try my patience by saying, 'UN meetings,' or I will kill you. I know you work for the Agency. In fact, I know everything about you. Save for the answer to my question."

I replied with one word, "Investigation."

"No. No, you are too junior to be conducting an investigation on my organization and our most important ass...asset," he replied angrily.

An air-conditioning unit kicked on and I felt a breeze across my nipples. It was then I realized, to my horror that, save for the hood on my head and the watch on my wrist, I was completely naked, my legs spread wide open, and my manhood left, well dangling.

"I'll tell you what, Señor Dong. You tell me why you are here, and not only will I let you live, I will make a place for you in HO. We can use a man with your predilections and redeeming feature," he had moved so close to me I could smell the Rioja on his breath: lush, fruity, with notes of menace.

"You said you weren't going to hurt him!" A voice called out from behind me. It was familiar, but I couldn't quite place it.

"¡Silencio!" Not so much a command as a bark. Someone was getting furioso, which didn't bode well for me.

"Look, I helped you get him here, but you said you were just going to ask him questions," the unplaceable, yet familiar voice whimpered. I heard the report of a heavy slap followed by a cry.

"Put a ball-gag on that one. No bag. I want him to see what his treason has wrought." Another barked command, and then I heard a struggle as someone was forcibly silenced.

"Señor Dong," Rioja-voice said, "HO has existed for over 2,000 years. It has penetrated every country's government and all of industry, to the highest level. We are not going to be taken down by some low-level Viet-Cong-Yankee-Doodle-Dandy hybrid when we own the Viet Cong and Uncle Sam!"

I wish I could do justice here to what this demented conquistador did to "Viet-Cong-Yankee-Doodle-Dandy," not to mention "hybrid," what with the lisp and the spit. There's no time for that because suddenly, he shouted something I had both wished for and dreaded.

"Take the bag off. I want him to see my face."

The bag came off. I wasn't surprised to find myself in a dungeon. Stone floors, gears, and hoists, abounded. Even with the bag on, I had felt the dampness and had surmised the floor was made of stone. Was this a dungeon-dungeon, or a sex dungeon? The sling in the corner answered my question. I also noticed my glasses on the nearby table. Was it a regular table, or a torture table? Then I noticed the straps and that answered that.

My captor looked like a cross between Antonio Banderas and Javier Bardem. The only difference was the green eyes that flickered beneath hooded lids, clearly some Nordic type once crash-landed in his family's gene pool. He wore a black suit, crisp white shirt, and a silver tie. His Castilian lisp gave him his own special brand of hotness.

Out of the corner of my eye, I caught one of his henchmen. He was, to my surprise, as naked as me and endowed with an impressive tool, though no competition. I'll call Henchman 1, Big Dick going forward. He had a HO tattoo on his left hand, as did the Spaniard. I could not see Henchman 2, but I knew he was there and that the tattoo would also be there. Branding in this outfit was not subtle. Somewhere behind me, the mystery man was sobbing, his ball gag doing a poor job of muffling the sound. Not that it was meant to. More likely, it was there to keep him from screaming obscenities, shouting for help, and ruining the villainous vibe. Which, in his shoes, I'd be doing too. Said villain now launched into a soliloquy to rival Cervantes.

"My name is Manuel Azramar and I am the head of the European branch of a society that existed before Christ walked this earth," he continued. "Long before the Crusades, and before the Americas were conquered, but perhaps you already know this," Azramar said. "What you likely don't know, is we have records of Homosexus Obsessi going back to the Roman Empire. Some believe it existed long before that, perhaps even in Sumeria."

I looked off in the wrong direction as he spoke.

"I tell you this," he droned on, "because we could provide a man with your... possession, and skill, a place in a world you've dreamed of, but have never walked in; the finest living accommodations, food, travel, your every appetite satiated. Men of your every desire spreading their willing holes for you at every turn, sitting atop your manhood and sliding all the way in. Pleasure at every turn."

Looking off in the wrong direction from where he stood, I replied, "I'm not interested."

"You say that, but your cock betrays you." He wasn't wrong there. My cock was already at half mast, but I was just horny. I don't have a particular fetish for dungeon sex, but one should never say never. He kept on, now teasing me. "It wants to penetrate nubile flesh. It desires hungry young mouths like Ilov's to drain it. I sent him to you, to talk to you. Did you desire that ass? Because it would be yours at my command. It would spread open for you, willingly."

It was all coming back to me. He was referring to the hot Bulgarian, Ilov Giandik, who, if I had to guess, slipped something in my drink that ended me up here, tied to this chair, and naked. I tried to think of taxes, war, debt, anything to make my cock go down. But it only got harder, longer, thicker. It was throbbing, as if it wanted to detach from my body and run rampant through the streets fucking everything willing and unwilling.

"Impressive indeed." He said, looking straight at my cock. He turned away and continued, "It would be Ilov's punishment for... subduing you. Though, I don't think he would consider it a punishment at all." And still, he went on. "In HO, you could be at the highest echelon based on your girth and length." He then added, obviously irritated, "I'm over here Dong. Why do you look there?"

"I'm sorry, I'm blind without my glasses," I said. Which is not anything James Bond would ever say were he in my situation. Where the gay Bond might say, "Shall I come to your room Anal Galore?" Here I was asking for my progressives.

"Oh for Christ's sake," he said. "All this theater is just lost on you." He grabbed my glasses and looked through them. "¡Dios mío! You are blind," he said as he slipped them on my face.

I immediately took in the surroundings, acting as if I was seeing them for the first time. With my spy glasses in place, I said the prompt and started running intel on my captor. Though all my captor heard me say was the statement, "You ought not to kidnap people."

"You should not travel to foreign countries under an alias," he replied, exasperated.

"Where's your pussy?" I queried.

"¿Qué pasa?" he asked, confused.

I said, "Every megalomaniac that heads a criminal enterprise strokes a long-haired, perfectly quaffed, picture-perfect white cat as he provides the hero, that's me by the way, with tons of exposition about his dastardly plans." My phone must have been in the room somewhere as it paired with my glasses and started sending me reports to view on one Manuel Azramar, a businessman originally from Salamanca, Spain but now residing in Madrid. At least he hadn't lied about his name, I thought.

"Oh, Señor Dong, you give me too much credit," he said with a sinister smile.

"Then they say that!" I added. "Or they say, you underestimate me." This I said in my best fake British accent.

"HO is not a criminal enterprise." He retorted. "We are the planet's, and its population's, best stewards. If our way of life is going to continue, we need Earth, and the people operating upon it, moving forward on all cylinders. We champion climate intervention. We fight a war on poverty. We work to end war, all in secret mind you."

"You've got to be kidding," I said. "A gay Illuminati?"

"Oh, my dear man," he said, now visibly perturbed—one hair shy of an offended clergyman. "The Illuminati only wishes they were as powerful as us. First rule of a secret society? Keep your secret society secret."

"And not all our members are homosexual, no. Some have wives—wives who cannot handle their appetites. Or their size. We offer these men an awakening. A liberation. Real pleasure."

He stepped closer, practically glowing now. His eyes burned with the zealotry of a prophet and the patience of a disappointed teacher.

"Really, Dong, do you think wars are fought for noble reasons? Empires don't rise and fall at the whim of gods. No! Kingdoms end because someone desired a very particular piece of ass. Paris of Troy? That was no love affair—it was lust, pure and thunderous. His monumental cock convinced Helen to abandon Sparta. Mark Antony? You think Cleopatra cared for politics? Please. It was his colossus that conquered Egypt, not his legions. And David, the psalmist-king? Bathsheba wasn't lured by poetry. It was the veined Goliath resting between those divinely sculpted thighs—that is what gave Israel its future.

I waited for him to catch a breath, but he didn't stop. He appeared to be part man, part manatee.

"It is not myth. It is record. It is law. Wars are cock-measuring contests, Dong. History is one long stroke-off. And men like you and me—gifted, chosen, hung like divine scepters—we are the rightful heirs to rule. Not because of votes. Nor virtue. Because of this."

He adjusted something beneath his suit.

I was starting to nod off. Thankfully, I had managed to hit the record button on my Agency-issued Inspector-Gadget wristwatch (my name for it, not the Agency's). There is no way I could remember this whole diatribe for my report later without it.

"But to be clear," he added. "To take over the world, well that would cost trillions of dollars. Never mind the destruction and death. We have no time or desire for that. So, instead we rule from the sidelines. We are well-placed coaches, mentors, and teachers. We influence, and in return, we are richly rewarded. "And if we don't do all this, well, we might lose out on ...him."

"Him?" I asked perplexed. "You mean some sort of gay Jesus?"

"Ja, ja," he chortled. "I can see where there might be a comparison, as some of our members say he might already be among us; 33% of our brethren want the man with the ultimate cock, while 33% want the man with the tightest, yet most expansive hole. The other 34%? They want him to have both."

Suddenly outraged. I yelled, "All this is just wrong, I mean morally!"

"Oh, spare me the lecture, Dong." He countered. "We do have a moral compass here at HO. We have our, and the world's, best interests at heart. Everything we do is for the greater good. Our ends justify the means. And if we have gods, they are Bacchus, or perhaps Eros." He then softened, sounding almost playful. "I hope you will consider joining us, Dong. My colleagues here can be very, er, persuasive," he turned acknowledging the two henchmen.

"Oh. Where are my manners? I failed to introduce you. These are my HO colleagues. You've already met Ben."

Big Dick nodded at me, his face impassive. I glared in return.

"He's the one that stripped you. This is his brother in arms, Tayl."

Tayl came forward from behind me. He too, no surprise, was also naked and well hung.

"You can thank him for the tightness of your restraints. You'll notice, like me, their HO marks are on their left hands, which signifies us as Power Tops. Bottoms wear their marks on their right hands. My intelligence tells me you are a top, as well. Of course, all that can change with a little spit and effort. But wouldn't that be a waste? Think it over, you too could sport a HO mark upon your left hand, Dong and keep your virtue intact."

I knew a threat when I heard one. Particularly when it wasn't veiled. It annoyed me that my hole responded with curiosity but also abject terror.

"Again, you ought not to hold people against their will in your dungeon." I said, as I looked straight at Ben and Tayl and their enormous cocks. The screen on my glasses started feeding me intel on the Czech, Ben Overntakit and the Frenchman Taylor Tapper.

"Dungeon?" he said, his accent making it sound like a place where orphans go for haircuts. "What better place to mete out your punishment? Unfortunately, I can't stay and watch the show, but I prefer it when the flesh is willing."

That sounded a bit ominous and actually had me worried.

"Have you reconsidered Mr. Dong?" he asked as he moved closer. I spat aiming for his face but hit only his crisp white shirt. Somehow, I had forgotten about the sucker-punch to my head, so the spittle was red with blood.

He pulled away a bit disgusted, but not as much as I had hoped.

"Good thing I wasn't going to be wearing this tonight," he said.

He undressed, slipping his suit jacket onto a hanger in a closet I hadn't noticed before. My own clothes hung beside his—neat, pressed, unnervingly domestic. He balled up the blood-spattered shirt and tossed it to the floor, then stepped out of his pants and faced me, unapologetic, lording his giant cock in front of my face. Still no competition, I thought. This said, my tongue tensed, wanting to flick out and taste him—like a tropical lizard eyeing prey just beyond its reach. He caught the look, gave a knowing half-smile, and turned away.

Now, I have many people in town and a function to attend. If you'll excuse me... and men, gag Dong as well, and show him no mercy. Start with Judas over there. He's of no use to us. I think the threat of your girth alone, Ben Overntakit, will have Dong coming over to the winning team in no time."

As he left, he looked straight at me and said, "Mark my words Dong, before your cock spews three times you will be joining HO, willingly."

Ben Overntakit glowered at me, while Tayl Tapper, fondled himself and gave me a wicked smile.

"That's rape," I started to shout but Tayl Tapper put a ball gag in my mouth. They then dragged the chair with mystery man in it from behind me and over to a table and strapped him down on his stomach. Spread eagle. He too was naked, and the ball-gag remained firmly in place.

Mystery man finally turned toward me as if to plead, I'm sorry. Oh no, it was him. I couldn't believe it, I thought.

He cried out through the gag as the first enormous cock went in, whether in pain or ecstasy, I couldn't be totally sure.

Chapter 2

It certainly didn't start this way. If anything, it was a routine, dare I say a banal, investigation. I got called into my boss's office, the chief auditor of the Agency, and I was given an assignment. The head of auditing, Mr. Gver, was a fairly fit, middle-aged man who wore too-tight polyester pants that barely contained his tool. The pants were a little shiny on one particular spot below his crotch, indicating an unusual wear pattern, as if it had been rubbed incessantly in that same spot over and over again. Any initial excitement I experienced about the assignment soon faded.

"I need you to investigate a particular secretary in the Agency. The software has flagged him," said Head Gver.

"A secretary general?" I said. "They never come our way. Thank you for your faith in me, Sir. I stammered. I won't dissap–"

"–sorry." the head interrupted me. "An administrative assistant to an Undersecretary. His expense reports are impeccable and unassailable on the surface. Too good to be true or certain. Anyway, the software has flagged it, and I need you to dig into everything. Well, let's say the last five years. I want you to be relentless. You ride his ass and you blow it wide open. We need some good PR down here."

Down here, referred to our dank basement offices in a nondescript, Washington, DC office building titled only "Agency," as the first half of the sign had been vandalized and never repaired. That part of the sign was long gone by the time I arrived to work here four years ago. Our department and IT were the only ones relegated to the slightly moldy-smelling basement.

"Got that Dong?"

"Yes, sir." I replied and left.

My colleagues Hugh G. Johnson III and Zitson Cox were snickering when I got back to my cubicle. Johnson was African American and the son of a Princeton economics professor. He was massive, weighing in at, I guess, 230-240 lbs. He was 6'4" and made of solid muscle. For the record, it wasn't just his biceps that were bulging. Gregarious by nature, he joined the Agency six months ago but already knew more people than me. He did a stint at the CIA as an agent, but unfortunately, had injured his back while on assignment in the field and needed a desk job.

Zitson Cox, on the other hand, had a Hungarian mother and an American father who retired from the diplomatic corps. Cox was about 5'10" dark hair and brown eyes with a perky butt. His mother ran the Agency's HR department. *Nepotism anyone?*

"Hear you got a big case Lucky Dog." Johnson guffawed.

Lucky Dog was a nickname that had been installed upon me when I was an exchange student in Wisconsin during my junior year of high school. It did not start out as a kind nickname, but rather a derogatory one as I, being of Vietnamese heritage, was teased relentlessly about the incorrect and racist dietary preferences of my people. If they only knew how good the food was compared to the tasteless meals my kind-but-bland host mother served me up during my exchange year. In the end, I took hold of the name like a badge of honor and owned it, thereby taking any power out of it. Plus, I prefer to be called Lucky Dog compared to my unfortunate birth name, Don Kee Dong, which inevitably caused relentless snickers and unwanted comments from adolescent-minded males when I first arrived in the U.S. Had I never left Việt Nam, I would have never known.

I spent the next two hours poring over the expense reports for one Phillip Mihol, the administrative assistant and his boss, the Undersecretary, who, like Johnson's father, had a Ph.D. in economics. Everything added up. No missing paperwork, no excess charges, no violations of agency policy.

I then looked up Mihol in the agency directory. He was young, mid-20s like me. He had an extremely handsome face hidden behind Clark-Kent-style glasses. According to his stats, he was 5′ 10", 159 pounds, blonde hair, and blue eyes. From what I could see, which wasn't much in the grainy photo, he was toned and, behind those glasses, pretty hot. He had also been working here longer than me. The directory indicated he was a nurse specialist in addition to being an admin. assistant and he had grown up in Amsterdam. You have to love international agencies, unbeholden to US personnel laws. You'd never find all this info on a good ole U.S. of A. company intranet. I don't get out of the basement much, but how had I never seen him before?

By the end of the day, after all that sleuthing, my brain was fried. I put in a request for access to their G drives so I could match the expenses with actual travel and closed out of my computer for the night. I needed to blow off some steam, so I headed down to the Metro and out to my favorite Korean spa in Arlington, Virginia. When I arrived at the spa, I checked in with my acquaintance Huang, as he's the evening attendant most nights. I got two towels and a locker key and headed in. I disrobed and hit the shower.

I was scrubbing myself down when I noticed a skinny white guy eyeing me. Well, actually, he was eyeing my package. I rinsed off, grabbed my towel, dried myself, and left my towel open when I passed him by, before I wrapped it around my waist and headed for the non-coed steam room. What can I say? I'm a showman.

As I approached the steam room, which Huang calls the "low-self-e-steam room," I hung my larger towel on the farthest hook and threw the smaller one over my shoulder. Low self-esteem? Maybe? All I knew is I was horny as fuck.

As soon as I entered all activity stopped. I sat down on my smaller towel. I moved my hand to my crotch, giving the universal gay-men's signal that I'm down for hijinks. Activity soon started and apparently I had interrupted a lot more than I initially thought, because the guy next to me went down on the girth of another and two guys I could barely see in the corner, who were covered by a shared towel... that's odd, I had initially thought... removed their shared towel and the one was mid stride in fucking the other. Usually, the guys in the steam room were just overly handsy. I guess more guys than me needed to blow off steam that night.

I sat back and enjoyed the show. The steam kicked off the thermostat when it, I guess, reached the temperature and or humidity setting. Now, I could hear all the hot sex noises more clearly, slurping, and hips on ass. My cock went full tilt. The guy getting head was moaning and the guy getting fucked just kept saying to his partner...

"Yeah, fuck me, fuck me harder."

My erection was still at 100%, when the door suddenly opened, and all activity once again ceased, and I failed at my attempt to cover my now massive cock. It was the skinny guy from the shower. He came and sat next to me and immediately grabbed my shaft and started stroking it. The others immediately took up where they had left off. Skinny guy had lube or spit on his hand because his strokes were mind-blowing. He then went down on my cock. He teased the head and went about halfway down my shaft, up and down, up and down. I laid back and I think my eyes may have rolled back in my head.

The guy giving the other guy head had been on his knees in front of him, but now he got on his knees on the bench next to me and resumed sucking the guy off. I now had a hot ass inches from my face, and the skinny guy going to town on my tool. I had one hand tangled in his hair, pushing his mouth on to more of my cock while, with my other hand, I started stroking and slapping the other guy's ass that was next to my face. His hole was hot so I started fingering it. Suddenly the guys fucking stopped. Everyone else stopped, panicked, and looked to the door, but it didn't open. Instead, the guy topping the other guy moved to the bench below me and plopped down his ass cheeks making a slapping sound on the wet surface. Meanwhile, the bottom he had been fucking moved to him and once again set down atop his shaft. He then started bouncing up and down on the fuck-cock. Skinny guy moved to accommodate, but he did not take his lips off my cock in doing so. The room was a pretty good size, but we were all crammed into a corner of it. If anyone had walked in on us before their eyes could adjust, they'd have trouble telling who was fucking who and who was sucking who. Six hot studs, their cocks just going to town.

Suddenly, one of the guys erupted in spasms. I felt hot semen first on my arm, then on my feet. Some more splashed on my face and in my hair as another one burst his nut. One by one the original four came. There was cum on the floor and bench, which made the room more dangerous than a slip 'n slide. Everyone came but me and the skinny guy. This said, the others did have a head start. They gathered up their towels and tried mopping up some of the spunk, but the lighting was too dim for them to do a thorough job. One by one they slipped out, leaving the two us behind in the half-lit room.

I took his hand, and we carefully left the room. I grabbed my extra towel on the way out and hung the small towel over my erect penis. It was a poor attempt at modesty. Skinny guy just laughed. As we passed through the shower, we cooled down and rinsed off. I then led him to a massage room in the back. Huang at the front desk, let me use it for just such an occasion. I led skinny guy into the room and locked the door from the inside. With a silent gesture, I directed him to the table. He understood, stretching out on his stomach without a word. The room smelled faintly of oil and disinfectant. I poured a slick ribbon of massage oil into my palm and worked it over his back, kneading, warming, letting my hands do the talking. When he turned his head to the side, mouth parted, I fed my cock into his mouth as he lay prone.

Then I whispered my first words to him. "Do you want me to fuck you?"

He purred and said, "Yes, please."

I immediately jumped on the table, my thighs on either side of him and my now half-hard cock poking him in various places as I slid up and down his backside. I massaged his shoulders as my hardening cock rubbed along his ass crack. I massaged his hot cheeks, sticking my finger and tongue gently into his hole. He moaned with pleasure. Then I stuck the head of my cock into his tight little hole and fed my length slowly, inch by inch until his hole understood what was going on and relaxed.

He started moaning and rubbing his cock against the table. Three minutes into the exercise, my cock was still only halfway in when he tensed up and came. I was disappointed as he orgasmed well before I could even get close to coming. I tried to keep my cock in him, as we really were just getting started, but he pushed me off him, saying my length hurt him too much. He thanked me, apologized, and left. My erection was throbbing.

I ended up jerking off onto my smaller towel, using his cum as lube. I headed to the shower, my head hung heavy, and I took a cold one.

I got dressed and left the spa, walking to a nearby Vietnamese restaurant called Nam-Việt. It was good to be among the familiar smells and language of home. The pretty kid working at the register always flirted with me. While cute, he wasn't my type. And further, he was way too young. His mother, or perhaps grandmother, wasn't there, which was weird as she usually was. The kid said she was in Việt Nam for a wedding. I was secretly grateful because she was always trying to show me pictures of eligible brides whenever I visited. Perhaps she had been successful in matchmaking another customer.

I filled up on my favorite dish, Bún chả Hà Nội, in English it would translate to Hanoi-style skinny noodles and grilled pork. It's so fucking good. Then I remembered skinny guy from earlier, and I lost my appetite. After pretty kid packed up my leftovers, I paid and then caught the Metro back to DC.

As I entered the warmth of my little apartment on 13th NW, I heard the friendly mewing of my little black and white tuxedo cat Mr. Bô Bô. As I climbed into bed with Bô Bô at my side, I lied to myself that tomorrow would be a better day.

Chapter 3

The next day, I got back from lunch early. I wasn't sneaking up on my colleagues, I guess I just wasn't that boisterous. Cox was standing behind Johnson, who was seated. Cox's crotch was pressed against Johnson's back.

As I came around the corner, I saw that Cox wasn't exactly giving Johnson a shoulder massage because he had his hands down his shirt, and his fingers may have been twisting his nipples. I gave a little bird whistle to announce myself.

Cox's hands flew out of Johnson's shirt and without missing a beat, he said, "How about that game last night?"

"I got that right here on video. Check it out," replied Johnson.

Wow, that Johnson's quick on the stick. I mean, he had the video up as soon as Johnson mentioned it, right? Once back in my cubicle, I opened my email and had confirmation that I had access to Phillip Mihol's and the undersecretary's G drives. This would give me unfettered access to all their folders. And it would leave no trace of my probing.

"I've got you by the ass Mihol," I muttered to myself.

Yet, by the end of the day, I had nothing. All the trips matched up with the expenses. Mihol's boss and Mihol traveled a lot. International conferences all over the planet. Mihol's boss was an expert on macro-economic social equity or some such bullshit. None of that mattered to me. What did matter to me was that I had invested a day and half on these bastards and I had nothing to show for it.

I barged into Head Gver's office, only to find him seated at his desk, while spasmodically rubbing up, back and forth, against the underside of it. Both hands gripped the sides.

"Yes, Dong," he yelled as he convulsed.

"Sir. Sorry to bother you," I stammered. "I found nothing on Mihol."

He said, "Hand me a couple of tissues. Would you?" As he breathed erratically and then softened to a more regular range.

I handed him two tissues, which were closer to me on the desktop than to him, I noticed his right hand was...moist with, hand cream, I think would be the best description. I pretended to ignore this and turned to my laptop and pulled up a screen. He did not blow his nose, and I didn't see what happened to the tissues.

"Everything checks out, Sir," I said, then quickly added, "For instance, on their last trip to Zurich, they stayed the exact length of the conference, and all the spending was up to snuff."

"Where'd they stay?" he asked suspiciously.

"It's called the Baur au Lac," I replied in perfect French. Never mind that Zurich is in the German-speaking region of Switzerland.

"What was the room class?" he countered.

"I don't know. It says LCS next to their rooms," I said, starting to get worried.

"You've got your laptop. Look it up," he said impatiently. "And look up the room's rate while you're at it."

"It's probably the Lakeside Corner Suite. It normally goes for 3,600 Swiss Francs," I said.

"And yet they paid 199 Swiss Francs." Head Gver said. "You don't think it's suspicious that they stayed in the finest hotel in the city in rooms that go for nearly four-grand a night for 199 francs!" The Head got more animated. "Does it seem extravagant? Perhaps even preposterous to you?" He moved on. "How did they get to the hotel from the airport?" he asked.

"A company called Swiss Top Transfer. It was 25 francs," I added quickly.

"Let's look it up." Gver said as he started typing away on his desktop computer. "Swiss Top... Hmm... here it is. "Redefines private, black car service, unparalleled luxury," for 25 francs. That's 21 bucks in US dollars. I don't think so!"

I paled. I failed to account for subterfuge. It was just looking at things on a surface level.

"Dong, I expect better from you!" Head Gver said loudly.

I was so embarrassed I fumbled, dropping my pen to the floor. I went down to get it and noticed a ridiculously large puddle of white, creamy stuff on the floor under his desk, with some crumbled up, weighted-down tissues next to it. Hand cream? I don't think so.

"Look, your time hasn't been totally wasted," he said with an almost fatherly tone. "You've been back and forth over these expenses. You know where they went, where they stayed, where they ate. Now, you just need to look it over with a more critical eye. While an Undersecretary can supplement their expenses out of their own pocket and make up the difference, it has to be on the paperwork and I don't see that here."

He stood up. There was a wet spot on his pants. Thankfully, his dick wasn't still out. I have no idea how he pulled that off, or rather, put it away.

"I expect to see some major progress by tomorrow," he said as he ushered me to the door.

I went back to my cubicle with my proverbial tail between my legs. Cox and Johnson said they were headed to a bar called the Green Lantern for karaoke and asked me if I wanted to go. It was the first time they invited me. I think the invitation had more to do with what I did, or did not, spy earlier than it did with officemate camaraderie.

"Perhaps another time, I told them, "Gver's on my ass and I need to... what do you always say Johnson? Get a dicking? Thanks though."

The Head stopped by my cubicle on the way out. "Don't stay too late, Dong," he said. I noticed the sticky wet spot was starting to dry as he made his way past me.

A few hours later, our janitor Ernesto stopped by my desk. "Hey Ernesto," I called out.

"You're working late, Mr. Lucky," he said, as he emptied my trash. Ernesto had been our janitor the whole time I worked at the Agency, and he was always kind to me, probably the kindest of anyone.

"Big project and the Head's all over my ass about it," I replied begrudgingly.

"If you don't mind my saying, I think he'd like to take his favorite big project and truly get it all over your ass." Ernesto said with a sly smile. "It might get you a big promotion."

"Well, that is never happening Ernesto. The promotion, or him touching this ass with anything," I said with a grin. "Goodnight" I added.

"Buenos Noches, Señor Don Kee Dong." he said, as he wheeled his cart away.

Out of curiosity. I went into Head Gver's office. His trash was empty, the tissues gone, the sploogey spot on the floor was clean and the office smelled of cleaning products. Gver might have cleaned it up himself, but I pretty much doubted that.

Chapter 4

I was awoken by Cox yelling, "What the fuck Dong! Did you stay here all fucking night?"

"I fell asleep in the middle of a spreadsheet," I said, as I wiped sleep from my eyes.

"Well, you've got indentations on your face from your keyboard. Seriously? I suggest you hit the showers at the gym next door, dude." Cox said.

I looked at the progress I made last night and I was impressed with myself. I hit save. Thankfully, my head on the keyboard hadn't erased anything. I did have to delete thousands of extra blank cells on the spreadsheet my forehead had likely created. Fall weather had descended on DC over the last couple of days so I put on my coat and walked to the gym next door. It wasn't my favorite, but as employees of the Agency, we all got free memberships. Fortunately, it came with towel and locker service. It reminded me a little of Huang's place. For a second, my manhood stirred, remembering the other night. However, when I remembered how it ended, I went flaccid.

I got to my locker. It was on the bottom, right next to this other guy's. I'm pretty sure he was gay. I thought to myself, why did they clump us all together? They should spread us out. I was bent over with the locker door open, when the guy dropped his towel seemingly by accident and exposed a pretty sizable dick. I sucked air at the sight of it.

He then said with a hungry look in his eyes, "I've never had Chinese food."

I seriously doubted this. Unfortunately, I and every other person of color in America is used to this racist bullshit. Whether he was making a brainless comment or wanted to fuck me just because of my ethnicity, didn't matter to me.

I simply looked him in the eye and said in my best Wisconsin accent, "Then you simply must try Chinatown Express in, of all places, Chinatown. Their Fuck-You-Too is delicious." As I slammed my locker door shut with too much force, I added, "Now you have yourself a good little day there."

Look, I'm okay with the fact that a person may or may not be attracted to me, but I don't think they should discount a whole race if not attracted or just want to have sex with me because I check a box. Either way, his loss, I thought.

I grabbed my towel and headed for the shower. I had my hair all soaped up when this brown-haired young guy with pretty eyes pulled back the curtain and said, "The showers are all full. Okay if I share yours?"

"You've got to be kidding. Serious?" I said as I rinsed some of the shampoo from my hair and looked out; he was right. "Is it because I'm Asian that you asked me?"

"No," he replied. "It's because you're hot and you're hung like a rhinoceros."

"Well, I was just leaving," I retorted.

"Please don't," he said. He closed the curtain and then tenderly touched my stomach, which ignited a fire in my crotch.

Soon he was on his knees taking in half my length. I fumbled with the plastic curtain trying to stretch it to the edges of the stall so we would escape notice as he slurped. It felt so good. His tongue flexing and flicking back and forth across my cock's head, slathering along my length. He occasionally took my cock out of his mouth and sucked my giant balls one at a time, then he managed to somehow get them both in his mouth at once. Next, he'd be right back on my cockhead. I could see his hot little ass cheeks as he sucked on my dick. I was imagining spreading those cheeks with my pole. I grabbed his head with both hands and tried to force more of my cock down his throat. He gagged and pushed me away.

"I'm not a fucking sword swallower, dickhead," he cried.

He quickly yanked the curtain back and left the stall. I found myself once again so fucking frustrated. It would be one thing if it had just been the guy from the other night and this one, but this was more than a pattern. I couldn't remember a time when I hadn't cursed my cock and my lot in life. It started with incessant teasing in primary school. When I popped a boner in front of the class for no apparent reason. The Lucky in my nickname came from the boys at my Wisconsin high school when they caught sight of my, "donkey schlong," as they called it, after PE in the showers.

I finished my shower, pulled on my work clothes, and made a detour for caffeine and carbs. I had earned a coffee and a bagel from the shop across the street, still warm from the toaster and I was hungry. Back at the office, I dropped my breakfast in my cubicle and called out a half-hearted "Morning" to Johnson, who was midway through roasting Cox about his now-infamous rendition of "Oops!... I Did It Again" by Britney Spears at karaoke last night. Johnson was relentless, Cox was blushing, and for a Wednesday, the place already felt offbeat enough to be interesting.

"Dong, you should have seen it." Johnson exclaimed. "He was thrusting his hips against the speaker. I thought he was going to bust a nut all over, but the boy never missed a beat." I faked a laugh to imply the camaraderie that didn't really exist between us.

I needed to take a leak, so I excused myself. The toilets were European style floor to ceiling stalls, which is odd in the States, but then we did work for an international agency. Their design left no gaps and featured a lockable door. There were just three toilets with a shared sink and hand-dryer on the wall. I couldn't pee right away. Despite believing I was alone in a private space, I was still cursed with pee-shyness. While I stood there, limp dick in hand, I heard the distinct voice of Head Gver in the stall next to me. These walls blocked eyes, not ears.

"That's it. Cox. Take daddy's cock in those sweet little lips of yours."

It was not my officemate, Cox, he was talking to. I had just left him back in the office with Johnson. I pressed record on my phone.

"Oh, you want some of this too, Johnson," He continued. "Let that nice Mr. Gver suck your big black cock, while Cox is slurping on mine. Oh, that's it. That's it," he said. Never mind that, One: it would be impossible to narrate a threesome with a cock in your mouth, even if you were a ventriloquist and Two: Johnson also was back in the office cubicles. Who was I to call his bluff? I continued along with my recording of Head Gvr's orgy of one.

"What's that Cox? You want to eat my ass out? Oh, yea! That's it. Eat that ass, get that tongue up in there." I could hear hand on dick going faster and faster, as his breath accelerated. "Oh, there she blows!" Yes, he said that. And I can prove it. "Fuck, yea! Fuck, yea! FUCK, YES!!!!!" He nearly yelled. I heard some flopping, gasping, sighing, then a flush, and the sound of the stall door opening, hands being washed, hand dryer on, hand dryer off, a throat clear or two, then footsteps fading away.

I shut off the recorder on my phone as I could finally pee. When I was done, I opened the stall next to me. It was incredulous. I saw, just as I had under his desk yesterday, a large puddle of white, creamy spunk on the floor and on the toilet seat. The Phantom Spunker had struck again!

Click went my camera on my phone. With the recording I had blackmail material, if I ever needed it. Little did I know I'd need it, sooner than later.

Chapter 5

Everyone went to lunch, save for me. So, I was alone when Ernesto started his shift. I told him there was a bit of a mess in the middle toilet stall, but that it wasn't me who had left it.

"Oh, I'm sure you didn't," Ernesto said. "That would be the Head's mess. Between you and me. I think that guy's got a sex problem. Three to four times a day. I have to clean up after him... but he does make sure I'm paid well. And besides, I sell it."

"What?" I stammered. "You sell it!"

"Do not say anything, por favor, mi amigo." Ernesto said. "But I package it up and I sell it to these rich gays here in the city and in Maryland. I think they mix it into their face cream. I tell them it is from the Georgetown lacrosse team. That it fights aging and promotes vitality. I have no idea... Gver giveth and I taketh it away. Mum's the word. I've got five mouths at home to feed." He put a finger to his lips and motioned a shushing sound, while he pushed his cart away.

On that note, I left for lunch and took the rest of the day off. Plus, I left my cat home alone last night and I needed to check on him. I went home, fed Mr. Bô Bô (who had been so happy to see me when I arrived), ate some leftovers from the other night, and watched my favorite old time movie *Casablanca*. Mr. Bô Bô was currently nestled on my lap. I was feeling sorry for myself and this old movie seemed to fit my mood. I mean, Bogart was rumored to have a huge penis, and in the end, he didn't get the girl. I joked to myself, had they made a gay-porn version it would be titled, *Cumblanca*. In it, Rick would be plowing Captain Renault with his pendulous cock, and taking advantage of their "beautiful friendship" to the hilt.

I bonked Mr. Bô Bô on the nose with my index finger and said aloud, "Here's looking at you kid." He just swatted back at my finger.

After the movie ended, I started a martial arts workout I was taught as a schoolboy in Việt Nam. As I went through the motions, I harkened back to the movie and the plight of the refugees in it as they tried so desperately to escape the impending war that was always hanging like dark threatening clouds overhead. I thought about how my mother and grandparents must have fought to survive the harrowing American War, as the people of Việt Nam referred to it. I had no idea how they did so, as they refused to talk about it if I ever asked.

After completing the workout, I climbed into bed and slept like a baby, Mr. Bô Bô at my side. I awoke, just before 5:00 a.m., to slimy underwear. I'd had a wet dream. I could only recall fragments—a hot blonde guy, blue eyes, and the most beautiful ass I ever beheld. The one thing I most remembered, my cock was fully in him. I rode him incessantly. He didn't complain. When you're packing like I'm packing, no complaining is the ultimate wet dream.

"Only a dream," I sighed. I then dumped my shorts in the laundry, fed Mr. Bô Bô, and got ready for work.

At 9 a.m., I had a meeting with the Head to present my findings. I had plugged all the expenses for Mihol's trips and those of his boss' into a spreadsheet. Along with those expenses, I listed what the costs should be based on normal prices for airfare, hotel transfers, and restaurants, etc. I loaded those into a pivot table so we could look at the data, every which way, not that we really needed to. Mihol was getting discounts of 80 to 90% on everything purchased. I checked the conference programs, but usually they weren't staying at the conference hotel. It didn't matter where they traveled to, Riyadh, Geneva, or Sao Paulo. Their travel was always discounted enough to fall into the Agency's per diems or other travel guidelines. First class tickets were reported at coach prices. Five-star luxury hotel suites were also reported at three-star discounted room rates. And the finest restaurants also served discounted meals. One might ask, "What's the issue?"

Typically, in cases of financial malfeasance, somebody's on the take. What favor was someone currying for these discounts? Was the Undersecretary also accepting bribes? Was Mihol a spy?

"Good work," the Head said. "I'm glad you got to the bottom of this, Dong."

"Sir," I countered. "We still don't know what's going on. If we really want to get to the bottom of what's up with Mihol and the Undersecretary, I need to pursue them into the field. They've a trip coming up in a couple of weeks to Budapest."

"Out of the question, Dong. We put a report together and we forward it to the Director General. That's our job."

"But sir, with all due respect, just a few days ago, you said I needed to ride his ass hard, that we needed some good PR down here. You know, a report will just get filed away. We need hard evidence."

"Absolutely not!" Gver retorted. "We've got plenty here."

"But all of this can be explained away," I scoffed. "We need pictures of them living large in first class, pairing filet mignon with the wrong wine and mispronouncing Niçoise in five-star joints.

"I don't know, Dong..." Gver said, but I sensed I was breaking through.

"We need eyewitness accounts of the hotel accommodations," I pressed. "Proof that they even attend the meetings, they say they attend. Maybe they don't even go on these trips and the expenses are bogus." I was confident this wasn't true, but I was running out of rationale. Perhaps, I shouldn't have provided so much damning evidence.

"Look, Don Kee Dong, it ain't happening. We don't go into the field. We're pencil-pushers. The Director General would never go for it."

I didn't want to do it, but he forced my hand.

"Well, what would the Director General think about a sexual harassment lawsuit?"

His eyes tracked me like a pair of blaring spotlights as I walked to the armchair by the window and sat, stretched my legs, clasped my hands behind my head, and struck my best impression of an arrogant blackmailer's pose. The kind of pose that says, "I hold all the cards and you're about to find out."

"What the hell are you talking about, Dong?" Gver barked.

"Well, nothing other than I heard three of my colleagues, my only three colleagues in this very department, having sex in the restroom stall yesterday morning." I knew Cox and Johnson weren't in the stall with him, but I had recorded evidence.

"That's preposterous!" He snapped. "Those kinds of allegations will get you fired, Dong." He kept repeating my name, holding back from calling me Ding Dong because he knew if he did I would walk him directly to HR and make him repeat it in front of Zitson's mom. In our outfit, going to HR is like going to the principal's office—no one gets out alive.

"Well, Dong, what's this about? Wasting my time?"

I wanted to say, it's about your ass is mine motherfucker, but instead I pressed play on my phone, having cued up the recording in advance just in case I needed it.

"You want some of this too, Johnson?" was all it took.

Moments later, a sweating Gver was on his knees, metaphorically speaking.

"So sorry to bother you, sir," he sputtered into the phone to none other than the Director General.

"We have a delicate situation," he continued as I listened in. "We need to look into something in Budapest. Probably nothing. But I need to send one of our analysts in for a few days. It will cost a bit more than usual. Deep cover. I'll send the expense waiver along with the request."

His temple pulsed as he shot me a look.

"What's that? Oh, Dong, Don Kee Dong.

He fell silent while the Director launched into a diatribe about that time when I did that one thing we don't talk about. To his credit, Gver waved off the Director's misgivings with impressive ease.

"Water under the bridge. Why he's one of our best men now, sir." I know he was lying about that part, I thought to myself, but I didn't care. Gver continued, "If there's a problem, I can assure you he'll get to the bottom of it. Plus, everyone else is busy."

He stopped to listen, his eyes on mine. I half expected him to make a face and stick his tongue out at me.

"Em, hmm...well, we, just, want you to be aware and able to control the narrative. As I said, probably nothing. But you know how you don't like surprises sir. Very well. Just a heads up. Thank you, sir."

Gver hung up the phone, turned to me with all the subtlety of a thousand tornadoes, and said, "Don't fuck this up, Dong!"

"I won't, sir. You can count on me."

At least my pledge was sincere.

Chapter 6

When my colleagues Cox and Johnson heard I was to be sent on a mission to the field, their attitude and demeanor toward me changed 100% for the better. True, they had warmed up to me a bit the other day, but now I was like the prodigal son returned.

Since Zitson's mother was Hungarian—picture Viktor Orban in come-fuck-me-pumps and strawberry curls—he said he would start educating me on Hungary, and Budapest in particular, beginning tomorrow morning. This he ended up doing with a zeal I had never seen from him previously. While he hadn't grown up there, he had spent a lot of time in the country as a teenager and was fluent in Hungarian, a language that he reported, has nearly zero relationship to any other European languages, save for a slight relationship to Finnish—a language spoken in a country from which Hungary is separated by a gulf and five other countries. How they share a related language, Zitson once said, was a great mystery lost to the ages. Also, a great mystery lost to the ages was how Zitson's mother came to run HR at the Agency, always answering the phone with the same three words: "We are listening..." which never failed to make the hairs on the back of my neck stand-up.

Meanwhile, as Hugh had once been a CIA agent, he said he would give me a crash course in spycraft and basic self-defense. Knowing I needed the former, but not the latter, I tried to get out of the self-defense training by citing his back injury. He wouldn't hear of it.

As Johnson already knew a lot of people at the Agency, including the Agency's field agents, he often tapped them for intel and, well let's say, other things. He quickly got on the phone and, in what he called his "white-guy" New Jersey accent, laced with lothario charm, said, "Bottoms, can you send me down one of those Italian glasses/watch/phone set ups, youse guys got up there? My man Dong is going deep over in Eastern Europe. Undercover, of course. I'd tell you more, but it's classified. Mmm..hmm, yes sir. Thank you kindly, Bottoms. Oh, and Dong is also going to need a U.S. passport with an alias and a credit card." He then turned to me, and covered the receiver. "What's a good name?"

"I don't know. Smith?" I said sheepishly."

"Something Asian, Dong. The first rule of spycraft is to fit in and never draw attention." I thought of my friend out in the burbs, actually my mind was blank otherwise. "Huang." I replied quickly, without much thought.

"How do you spell that?" he asked. I wrote it down for him. "Tell you what, I'll give you an American-sounding first name. It was my great uncle's."

Soon he was speaking back into the receiver. "The cover name is, Horace Huang, H-U-A-N-G. Got that? Good. So how long will that take? Okay. Oh, awesome. Don't forget, I'm going topside on you, next Thursday. Yea, you can bring the passport then. Later gator," he said, and then he hung up.

I had to admire Johnson. He had them lined up like a daisy chain, nearly every night of the week.

"The gear and the credit card we get shortly. The passport we get next week. Which I will collect, personally," he said with a sly smile.

Soon after, four discreet packages arrived down the Agency's antiquated vacuum tube system addressed to Johnson. Out of the first he pulled my new credit card, which he handed to me. It was embossed with my cover-name and read, Diner's Club International. It looked fancy. Because this wasn't my real name, it also looked stolen. I grimaced and probably looked complicit and guilty.

"What?" Johnson asked perplexed. Then he grumbled, "It's your new name and you need to own it in less than, what is it, ten days?

The other packages contained a pair of pretty cool glasses, what looked like a designer watch, and a mobile phone which when I turned it on, read across the screen 'Hello Moto.'

Johnson paired all three and then said, "This is military grade shit. German-engineered with an Eye-talian flair. You won't find this sexy-looking type of gear over at the CIA." I'm sure Frank Sinatra was spinning like a scratched Capitol Record in his shallow grave at Johnson's pronunciation of Italian.

The phone looked standard issue low-tech, but had a hidden full keyboard, with Windows access. While the glasses, per the instructions, had a built-in display screen, visible only to the wearer, a camera, and night vision. They also went dark when exposed to sunlight and had an anti-fog coating. The watch had a recording device, and all the items had all kinds of other hidden features.

When I put the glasses on my vision was super blurry. I immediately removed them. "I can't see out of these," I protested.

"That's because I haven't synced them to you, yet," Johnson said. He took them and entered some keystrokes on the phone, and then had me put them on again. "Put them on and tell me when your vision is perfect."

I signaled when I could see super crisply and he said, "If anyone else wears them, they'll be blurry and they won't be able to see a thing."

"Why would anyone else wear my glasses?" I stammered.

"I don't know. But it keeps them from seeing the built-in tech," he replied. "Now, I need a trigger word when you want to run intel. You ought not to use a word that you might say in normal speech."

"Ought not?" I asked while still wearing the glasses. "I've studied and spoken English for over half my life, and I've never said, ought not."

Suddenly there was a ding and a computer voice in my ear, "Trigger word selected and stored."

"I didn't choose a trigger word," I protested.

"Yes you did. It's actually two words. Ought not is your trigger phrase. You said you've never used it, so that makes it the perfect trigger phrase. You won't accidentally say it. Try it now," he directed me.

"Ought not," I said while looking straight at Johnson. In a second or two at most, right before my eyes, in block letters, the name Hugh G. Johnson, III appeared along with his picture and the words, Princeton, NJ, USA – Former, Washington DC – Current, CIA operative – Former. Groin injury – Medically discharged. U.N. Specialized Agency – Current.

"It says you have a groin injury," I said.

"Give me those!" He said as he attempted to rip them off my face. They didn't budge.

"Ow!" I protested. Then "Cool." They were literally cemented to my face. "Nice tech!"

"Zip it Dong. Mums the word on my injury."

Just then Cox approached the back table where we were working. I turned to look at him, when the glasses reported, 5'10", MALE, APPROACHING FROM LEFT REAR on the view screen.

Johnson, always quick on his feet, changed the subject. "Now let me know when you can see Cox naked with the X-ray feature."

Cox dropped his hands to his crotch and turned beat red.

I wouldn't have minded getting a gander at Cox's cock, though I had more than once taken a long gander at his perky butt. Sometimes those wiry bureaucrats can surprise you with a plum-headed perfectly curved cock or delicious tight hole. But interoffice sexcapades weren't really my thing. Once out in the field I promised myself I would be more adventurous where the entanglements were easier to disentangle. Try as I might I could not see past his hands.

"They don't have that tech...yet," Johnson said, cracking up.

"I was just coming to see if you guys wanted to grab lunch," Cox said, a bit flustered.

At last, a lunch invitation. What had changed? It had to be the new mission. Or did Cox know something I didn't. Was this the last meal of the condemned? I chose not to question it. There will be plenty of time for questions in the future.

"That would be great," I said. "By the way, where's Gver?"

Ugh, I just couldn't help myself. There are always follow up questions. This is going to be my new spy's life, question everything. My motto going forward will be: Anticipate, Interrogate, Penetrate, and get the hell out. It will work on the job, and on dates.

"He said something about a sudden family emergency in an email he sent us a few minutes ago," answered Cox. "He'll be gone for the rest of this week and most of next."

Johnson looked up from the gizmos which was the name we settled on to call all three.

"Cool. He's always breathing down my neck. The guy gives me the creeps and he's always rubbing his dick. You ever noticed that?"

"Not at all!" Cox and I said simultaneously, then both of us burst out laughing.

"Did you mention lunch?" I asked.

"Yes! Let's go get some grub," Cox said.

"But Dong," Johnson said. "This afternoon, and for the rest of the week, we are going over how to conduct yourself covertly in the field and how to get people to lower their guard.

On Monday, we teach you some basic hand-to-hand combat skills."

That gave me a sure-fire boost of confidence. While I may be lacking in the spycraft department, H-to-H, was one area in which I was never lacking.

Chapter 7

Monday morning at 7 a.m., Johnson and I met at a sparse gym near the Navy Yard in what looked like, on the outside, an abandoned warehouse but was in actuality a hub of activity on the inside. It was *intimate*, in a way only hyper-masculine spaces can be, where violence pressed up against admiration, where sweat mingled with curiosity, and unspoken things rippled across the room under the cover of drills and discipline. I was dressed in loose sweats as instructed.

"What sort of place is this?" I asked.

"It's an FBI training facility. A buddy of mine lets me use it from time to time. Mostly, I just work on rehabbing my, eh, ah, shoulder."

"I thought it was your groin?" I noted. Later, he would confide in me that his on-the-job groin injury resulted from his interrogation of a hot Russian mole. He said, under no circumstances, was I ever to divulge this to Zitson Cox. I assured him I never would, but I could not vouch for the Russian mole. He said, as long as Cox avoided seances it would not be a problem.

"You ask too many questions and remember too much, Dong," he said.

"Which I guess makes me a good spy." I quipped.

"*Will* make you a good spy. You are far from perfect in this area. Don't get cocky!" he said. He then motioned with his hand towards the door and said, "In."

Johnson checked us in with the guy at the desk, the desk was behind thick, I assume, bullet proof glass. "He needs a sparring set, a *full* sparring set," Johnson said with an emphasis on the word full, as he pointed to me.

I was then handed a little worse-for-wear foam helmet; foam hand and foot guards; shin guards; an external groin protector; and thankfully, a new mouthguard. I looked at it all, and asked Johnson, "Do you seriously think I need all this?"

"Yes, yes I do," Johnson said matter-of-factly.

"What about you?" I queried.

"I have my own equipment," he said. His equipment turned out to be half of what I was just issued. We were then buzzed into the facility after leaving both of our IDs with the attendant.

We made our way toward a central chamber with high ceilings and skylights above, and a series of offices or perhaps other sparring rooms on the higher floors. There were eight huge thick red mats on the floor, half of which were already occupied by two guys each sparring and an occasional coach. There were benches around the perimeter of the room, some with bags and gear on them. We made our way to an empty one and set our bags and gear atop it.

I had never used this kind of equipment back in Việt Nam, so Johnson had to help me get it on.

"Hands last," he said as I began to put them on first.

"Ouch!" I said as he was helping me get the groin protector on.

"Adjust yourself to fit," he said.

“Easier said than done,” I quipped.

Once I was geared up, he quickly put on his headgear and foam hand and foot guards. We walked over to an empty mat. Johnson then said, "Let’s spar.”

“Come at me,” he said, his voice low just for me. I was breathing hard. He wasn’t. His breathing was even, controlled, eyes locked on mine. He shifted his weight, one foot sliding back with a whisper against the mat, his hips angling just slightly. His hand rose slowly—fingers loose, palm open, and then he curled them inward, one by one, in a slow, deliberate beckon, the kind meant to draw you closer, not chase you off.

I went toward him, feigned to the left, and then as he went to grab me, I doubled back and had him on his back with a thud. It was quick, bloodless. Just the way I liked it.

Silence reigned down across the facility, even from the floors above and I felt every head turn our way.

“Where the fuck did you learn to do that?” He implored through gritted teeth, as he winced.

“In gym class...at my Russian school...in Việt Nam,” I replied.

Soon, there was a line to spar with me. Some hot, some not. I removed the awkward gear (the groin protector) and kept only that which was necessary (head and hand gear). No matter the challengers’ sexiness, one by one I dispatched them. There was one guy who gave me a run for my money. His fighting technique? Krav Maga, developed by the Israeli Defense Forces. It took some fancy footwork which included a risky kick to the throat which left my balls vulnerable to a hammer-fist strike, but the gamble paid off and I took him down.

Another guy lingered a little longer than normal when I had him pinned down, my cock necessarily pressed against his ass. I swear he undulated a few times with his hips pressing against my massive tool. When we finished, he gave me his number, saying he'd like to "spar" with me again.

Afterward, we hit the showers. What the facility lacked in charm, was made up for by all the steamy masculine energy. Guys stood around naked, one with his foot on a bench, his ox balls dangling. They joked with one another, occasionally asses were slapped. In the open shower, super fit guys occasionally washed each other's backs. It immediately took me back to high school and the words flashed through my mind, DANGER... AVERT EYES!!!! I could not afford to get a hard-on here. I walked in with Johnson, we both hung our towels and Johnson gave a low whistle.

"You gotta license for that thing Dong?" he said with admiration while looking at my cock. "At least now I know why they call you Lucky."

How ironic, after I had just been cursing it the other day. I just asked, "Why are you looking at my cock?"

"It's kind of hard to miss, Dong. Like if a stallion suddenly walked into the showers here, no one is going to ignore it," he said matter-of-factly.

I looked to his very impressive tool, which heretofore, I had been trying to ignore and said, "I'm sure you get no complaints," raising my head in a quick motion to indicate his cock. "And you've got them lined up for miles."

"Yea, but with that cock of yours, I'd have 'em lined up to California. You must be the happiest man alive," he said.

"Something like that," I said. "Now, let's hit the showers or we're going to be late to work."

All talk and jokes stopped when we walked into the showers and, once again all eyes turned.

Later as Johnson and I approached the Metro to head to the office, I forgot all the dick talk and was feeling rather smug and, true to Johnson's words, the happiest I'd been in a long time, though for a different reason. "Thank you!" I proclaimed. "That was fun!"

"Yea, I think we can skip additional hand to hand training and focus on your spycraft, which I might point out is very lacking," Johnson said this as he rubbed his back. By 9 a.m. we arrived at the office and to an inquisitive Cox. "How'd it go?" Cox asked. "Dong's in one piece. So, I guess well?"

"Let's just say, he mastered H to H in one morning, but he still lacks proper spycraft," said Johnson.

"Not my fault you keep coming up with random one-off techniques that you suddenly recall," I said, still feeling a little defensive after my multiple battles.

"If you feel you can proceed with outdated methods, be my guest," Johnson said.

"No, no," I quickly responded. "Spycraft training it is, all you want."

"I'd like to see a little gratitude for my efforts," Johnson added.

"Of course," I said, without thinking. I will kiss your ass until the cows come home, but you are not going topside on me with that enormous tool, I thought.

Chapter 8

I arrived in Budapest at noon local time seven days later. I left Mr. Bô Bô with Cox. They had bonded immediately, which I must admit made me a little jealous.

I managed to convince the Agency to let me fly business class because they wouldn't go for first class. I pulled Mihol's and the Undersecretary's travel itinerary, so I flew on the same flights. They were booked in coach, but seemingly by magic they ended up in first class. I had booked one of the aisle seats in the first row of business, so I would be able to view the first-class cabin. I managed to get a good look at them while craning my neck and took a quick photo with my cool new glasses. Mihol looked back just then, but I was sure he didn't notice me. I was, however, caught looking into the cabin by a male flight attendant. He brusquely closed the curtains. I noticed a tattoo on Mihol's right hand when I zoomed in on the photo, I think it read HO, but I couldn't be sure as it was a bit blurry.

I carried my luggage on, but Mihol and the Undersecretary just had briefcases. I followed them at a subtle distance as they exited the plane. They went through the diplomat line at border security. But, as I was traveling undercover, I went through regular security. That's how I lost them. The agent looked at me queerly when I handed him my US passport. He was solidly built, 6 foot 2 inches, maybe 175 pounds and he had piercing green eyes.

"What is your business in Hungary, uhm... M... Mr. Huang?" he asked in halting English.

"Conference," I said. I tried to rush him but then realized that it seldom works. I just didn't want to lose Mihol and the Undersecretary in the airport's crowd.

"Will you be staying in Buda, or Pest, or somewhere else?" he queried.

"What?"

"It is a simple question, sir." He retorted, looked at my brow then settled his eyes uncomfortably on mine. What tell-tale signs was I giving off.

"I'm staying at the Intercontinental," I said, hoping that would answer his question.

"That would be on the Buda side of the river, sir." He went on to add. "Might I suggest you take a bath, sir?"

"Excuse me?" I asked, incredulously.

"Budapest is famous for its medicinal baths. Might I suggest Rudas Thermal Bath. It is, how you say, men-only tonight. 19:30 is an excellent time to go. Have a nice visit to Hungary, sir," he said with a tight-lipped smile. He stamped my passport and motioned me to move along.

I quickly made my way to baggage claim. But there was no sign of Mihol or the Undersecretary. How had their luggage already arrived? I thought. I assumed I missed them. I went to the exterior island where the hotel informed me, I would be met by my driver.

"Huang, Mr. Huang," This handsome guy holding a sign with my cover identity's last name said, looking right at me. How'd he know it was me? I thought. Then I looked around–yep, only Asian guy in sight.

"That's me," I said.

I seated myself in the back of the stylish Mercedes with plush leather seats, as the driver stowed my luggage in the trunk. Nice perk. Free limo service to and from the airport. With the door closed the car was completely soundproof. As he passed my window I noticed for, the first time, that the driver was hot! What was it with these stunning Hungarian men? I'd only encountered two and of course passed hundreds in the airport and now I was practically salivating. This guy had an athletic build, shortly cropped brown hair, and smoky gray eyes.

"Huang is an interesting last name. Are you Chinese?" He asked as he maneuvered us out of the airport.

"No. American." I retorted. Which was kind of a dick thing to say, so I quickly added, "but my people come from Việt Nam." Johnson said, field rule number one, don't make waves and don't draw any unnecessary attention to yourself.

By my people, I guess I meant me too, as I was born and raised in Hà Nội. But saying I was American matched my cover identity and technically I was here as a spy. So, I needed to be covert. I repeated the story in my head that had been drilled into me by Johnson: I am Horace Huang. I am a pharmaceutical rep from Wisconsin in Budapest to attend meetings of one of over a dozen UN-affiliated agencies, as my company has interest in the current treaty negotiations, or so the story went.

"My name is Yuri. Yuri Gettinlaid. I work for the Hotel Intercontinental," he said. Well, his employer was who I thought it was, but I guess he could have worked for an outside car service.

"I thought you were like Bruce Lee. You are very fit," he said.

"I eat right, exercise, try to get eight hours' sleep," I replied. I heard myself oversharing but couldn't stop. At least I sounded normal. A real spy would've just grunted a response. I sounded like a true Midwesterner.

"You'll like the hotel. It has a full gym. It's nice. You can also use cars, not just for coming and going to the airport. We have a small fleet." A beat later, he added. "See that car just ahead. It's one of ours. I can tell because the circular decal on the bumper is part of the hotel logo."

I peered at it, and guessed, as they were also staying at the Intercontinental, that my targets were in that town car. The logo on the bumper was subtle. It was just the letter "I" ringed by laurel leaves on the sides. The car ahead suddenly made its way toward an exit.

"Why aren't you following them?" I asked a bit panicked.

"That's not the way to the hotel," Yuri said.

Knowing, from my lessons with Cox, that money was very dear here, and the cost of living was much lower than in the U.S. I quickly asked, "if I give you 20 US dollars, will you follow them?"

"Of course," he said without a second to consider. He moved the car safely over and exited behind the other car.

"Don't make it obvious," I said. The car pulled up to a building in a somewhat industrial area. "Stay back here, please," I suggested. Mihol exited the car and went into the building.

Not able to read Hungarian, I asked, "What's that store?"

"That one is a copy shop," he said as he pointed and then he trailed off.

"The one he just went into, what is it?" I asked a bit more irritated than I had planned.

"Well, next door is, how do you say, an American-style adult superstore." He seemed pleased with himself. Then he added, "or you could call it a sex shop: dildos, lube, arse plugs..."

"Yea, yea, I get it," I said.

Mihol walked out only a few minutes later and loaded a black duffel bag into the trunk. He wasn't there long enough to shop, instead he had picked up an order. Then he went into the copy shop and came out carrying a box that he also placed in the trunk. He was in the copy shop longer than the other place. Mihol got back in the car, which was identical to ours, and it pulled away.

"Wait a minute," I said. After about 30 seconds passed, I said, "Okay, let's keep following them. There were no further stops and both cars ended up at the Hotel Intercontinental, Budapest. I gave the driver 30 U.S. Dollars to include a tip, and put my index finger to my lips in what I hoped was the international signal of mum's the word.

He nodded, "Please call me if you need a ride anywhere in the city... I give you my personal mobile here on this card, sir." I thanked him, stuck the card in my back pocket, and moved toward the lobby. I wheeled my luggage behind me, declined the doorman who tried to take my bag. "It has wheels," I thought. "I'm good." Once in the lobby, I lingered behind a pillar within earshot of the front desk, but out of sight.

"Herr Professor and Herr Mihol, welcome back to the Hotel Intercontinental." The front desk clerk said in a fawning manner. "Your suites are prepared as you requested, your luggage is already unpacked, and your clothing pressed. Francois here will show you up." The Undersecretary and Mihol nodded, but neither uttered a word.

After they followed the bellhop to the elevator, albeit with no luggage, I approached the desk with a smile and a can-do attitude. I expected a similarly warm greeting, but all I got was, "Do you have a reservation here?" as the clerk eyed me up and down with an air of distain.

Alright buddy, I clocked the clerk: gaunt, florid face; eyes cold and pale hovered above his bifocals; shoulders up to his ears; mouth set in a hard line; hands trembled. It didn't take a master spy to see this guy was more pest than buda.

It also wasn't lost on me that the 'here' in the welcome, if one wanted to refer to it as such, was not necessary, and perhaps implied that I did not belong, "here."

"Huang," I replied. "Horace Huang." The clerk looked quizzically at me. "And yes, I do have a reservation, *here*." I said the last word with an unusual emphasis, which was likely lost on him.

"Well, Mr. Huang," he said almost contemptuously, "I have you in one of our river-view rooms. Credit card and passport, please."

"Why?" I asked. "The last guests were just ushered to their rooms, with no formality."

"Why? Because you are you, and they..." he said beamingly, and then just as quickly his disposition turned to menace, looked down his nose at me, "are...not you. They, in fact, are our most honored guests..."

I handed him Horace Huang's passport and credit card. The Agency can be a mind-numbing bureaucracy, but when you need a credit card in a fictitious name in less than an hour, they can deliver absolutely, positively, faster than overnight.

"Everything seems to be in order," the desk attendant said with a note of disappointment. "The lifts are to your left. Next, please." I turned as I made my way to the elevator, luggage in tow, expecting to see another guest, but there was no one behind me.

Chapter 9

I had chosen my hotel room, in part because of its view of the Danube River, but mainly because it offered a view of the hotel's main entry point. About 5:00 p.m., I saw my driver, Yuri from earlier, while he held the door open for Mihol and the Undersecretary. They drove off. I waited a few moments and then I called the driver's mobile number. The phone rang, and he answered.

"Hello, this is your guest from earlier, Horace Hung,"

I said. "Do you speak Russian?" I asked in perfect Russian. As a former resident of the USSR, I assumed he might.

"Da," he said.

Our conversation continued in Russian, "I can tell you are in the car now. Where you headed?"

"A very fancy restaurant." he responded.

"Oh, which one?" I queried.

"It's called Babel, he said."

"Is it far?" I asked, cognizant that I peppered him with questions.

"No, it's close. Do you need a ride somewhere?" he asked.

"Yes, yes I do," I replied.

"I'll come get you. Call guest services and tell them you want Yuri to take you," he directed. "Now tell me, how is it that you speak Russian like a native?" he asked.

"I'll tell you when I see you. I thanked him and said goodbye, "Spasibo...Do svindaniya," I said as I disconnected.

I called the front desk and then went downstairs and waited and waited. Finally, I got a text from Yuri. It read, "Sorry. One of the gentlemen needed a ride somewhere else. Please ask another driver to take you." I did as I was instructed although the restaurant was so close I could've walked.

I arrived at Babel and explained to the host that I was meeting someone. The host responded, "May I ask the name of the party?" I gave the Undersecretary's last name and the host pointed to the table. Thankfully the restaurant was busy, so the host immediately lost interest in me and moved to his next task.

It was a small restaurant. I surveilled the Undersecretary's table, but Mihol was nowhere in sight, which was to be expected given the last text I'd received. While I pretended to look at my phone, I took pictures discreetly of everyone sitting at the Undersecretary's table with my spy glasses. They were distracted by their wine and appetizers and did not notice me. I then crossed the room, wary of the staff, but thankful for the restaurant's busy nature, and took pictures of the other guests at the table from another vantage point. The glasses provided me with the names of the other diners at the table as well. Those would be saved on my phone automatically, which would be handy for my report later.

I then made my way towards the exit and lied to the host that I was going out for a cigarette. Not an unusual statement given the number of people I noted smoking on the street when I arrived. I of course never returned.

I was hungry however; I just wasn't going to eat there by myself. Instead, I made my way down along the Danube River until I reached Central Market Hall, a vast multi-storied food market crowded with visitors. There was beautiful fresh produce, hung dried peppers, and mouth-watering cakes. Zitson told me about it and said it featured both fresh and prepared food, as well as souvenirs. He also said it was not to be missed.

I purchased a half rotisserie chicken covered in paprika, the Hungarian equivalent of French fries, and a soda from a vendor's stall on the second floor. It truly was a "Value Meal." It was so cheap and so good. Once done, I texted Yuri, but I received no response. It was 7:00 p.m. and I was at a dead end. Then I suddenly remembered what the border agent back at the airport suggested.

I spoke my prompt, then said, "Look up thermal baths," to no one in particular, but the gizmo picked up my query. It listed a few options on the view screen. The name Rudas rang a bell since it was the one I thought he mentioned. I then asked for directions and was pleasantly surprised that it was located back along the river towards the hotel and just across one of the many bridges. So, with nothing left to do here, I decided to take in more of the local culture and customs.

Chapter 10

I arrived at the Rudas Bath and was immediately hit with the smell of sulfur. Not my favorite smell, but it meant this bathhouse was built atop a legit natural spring. I checked in with the attendant. It too was so cheap! For under $20 I got access to the thermal bath and a 60-minute massage. I was stressed and I was worth it.

I was handed a locker key attached to an ugly yellow-elastic-spiral wristband and, of all things, a beige apron and was instructed via hand gestures how to wear it. It looked like those nail aprons worn by hardware store employees or by a contractor. It had big pockets at the waist to carry a tape measure or nails for a contractor. What the pocket's purpose was for here, I had no idea. This wasn't a sex club after all. At one of those, the guys would love a handy place on their person to store their lube and poppers, etc. When I asked for a towel first in English, then in Russian I was told I could trade in the apron for a towel when I was ready to leave the bath.

I undressed at my assigned locker and tied the apron around my waist. The bath reminded me a bit of my friend's place in Arlington back in the DC suburbs, and at the same time it was very different. For one, it was ancient and beautiful. I felt stupid wearing the apron but most everyone was wearing one though some were completely nude.

Perhaps their apron was nearby. I saw some guys wearing theirs, so it covered their cock and balls. That would not work for me, as half my cock would hang below the hem. I saw another guy sitting on his apron, which kept his ass cheeks from coming into contact with the marble bench he had perched himself atop as he engaged in a deep conversation. Whatever he was talking about it involved lots of hand gestures.

Then I figured out the perfect purpose for the pocket, at least for me. This came to me when I noticed my apron had a small hole in the back of the pocket. When no one was looking I tore it bigger and then fed my length into it. Now that I was contained, I made my way to one of the pools and stepped in. The water was hot and nice. There were only men in the pool, as promised. Some were sitting in the water, some were alone and others were in small groups talking. It was intimate, but not sexual. Or had I thought this too soon? I felt someone swim between my legs and caress my ass as he did so.

He popped up and said, "I'm so happy you came." There in his 6-foot, 2-inch frame, washboard abs, and an estimated 175 pounds of Hungarian glory was the border agent from the airport. Hairless chest and ripped all over.

"Hello, officer," I said.

"Please. I'm no longer at work," he said. "You can call me Dominik, Domnik Thisass, Domo for short. Come swim with me," he motioned. We swam over to a dark corner of the pool. "You are so exotic," he said. "As soon as I saw you, I wanted to kiss you." As he said this, he grazed his fingers across my stomach. How did guys instinctively know that this move gives me an instant erection?

"I bet you say that to all the Asian boys." I quipped. Then added, "You're making a few assumptions there pal. To start, how do you even know I am gay, that just because I'm Asian, I'm...?" He interrupted me.

"Your apron tells me the real story" he said this as he grabbed my hard cock and led me to a dark corner of the pool.

"Can't fool you," I said as I arched a rakish eyebrow. He smiled. Then he put his lips to mine and we kissed. It was amazing—my Hungarian god. Next thing I knew, we were in an even darker corner, and I was seated on a ledge, the apron under my ass, my cock out and engorged. He was in the water, going to town on my tool. It barely fit in his mouth, but that didn't stop him from taking it halfway down his throat. Soon he was standing over me. His back was to me and his beautiful hard cock and hairless balls were bouncing around over my head, while the perfect globes of his ass were parting like the Red Sea in front of my eyes.

He leveraged his body by grabbing some protruding rocks above our heads and presumably keeping an eagle-eye out for any observers. He then began to rub his hole against my mouth. I was in ass heaven as my tongue started forcing its way into his puckering tight little hole.

In between tongue-dives, I dug my fingers into his willing flesh, prying his hole further open and driving my tongue deeper. He moaned. Once I had his hole nice and wet with my spittle, he turned around with his hard cock facing me, I quickly put it in my mouth, but not for long, as he soon squatted down upon my engorged prong taking his cock, now covered in my spittle, with him. I felt the head of my cock disappear and a few inches of my length go in.

He was going up and down still using the rocks above me as handholds. Had he done this before at this very location? Was this his routine? Single us out at customs, make a date for the bath, lure us to the dark corner of the pool, grab the rocks and fuck us until we're begging for a wedding ring—or at least an extended stay and work visa?

As soon as I asked myself this, I realized I didn't care. The idea of what was happening and where it was happening, coupled with his absolutely stunning good looks, was just so hot. And while it was hot, and I did not complain, he was literally only putting half of my cock in at any given time. I tried to push him down further onto my manhood by grabbing his hips and trying to force him down, but he was the one in control.

We were kissing and his hard cock was poking me in the stomach up and down, up and down, and then his hole clenched, and with moaning gasps pushed into my mouth like the breath of life, he spilled his seed all over my stomach. When his waves of pleasure subsided, he kissed me again, more passionately than even before.

"You are so beautiful," he said as he stood up, pulling me out of him as he did so. He then jumped backwards, feet first into the water, pulling me in after him. He stroked my length a few times, until we were interrupted by the electronic squawk of a rusty loudspeaker.

"Number 69," was called out in English. I then realized that someone had been yelling something in Hungarian earlier but not knowing what they were saying I had ignored it. A bunch more squawking came over the loudspeaker. I understood #69 in Russian, then in English. He pulled up my wrist where the yellow spiral-coiled wristband with a key and the number 69 appeared.

"Did you order a massage?" He asked.

"Yes," I replied.

"Well, it looks like your number's up," he said. "You better go. They get very angry if you keep them waiting. I hope you don't get Sergey. He's the meanest of them all." He kissed me. "Perhaps we can meet here again. The day after tomorrow, at the same time?" he said. Then he kissed me one last time and swam away.

I quickly shoved my cock back through the apron hole and then swam towards the shallow end of the pool. Once there, I was greeted by a hostile, stoutly built Hungarian, wrapped in what could only be called a loincloth or what a sumo wrestler might wear, but he wasn't as big as a sumo. He said something in Hungarian. I asked if he spoke English. He did not respond. He just asked, "Number 69?" in English. Then he added, a bit miffed, "We call and call you."

I put on my best fake-Midwestern smile, offered my hand as if to shake, and said, "I'm Horace Huang."

He did not take my hand; he just looked confused.

"That's my name, Horace Huang," I offered, still retaining the fake smile.

"Okay, Horace. I'm Sergey," he responded matter-of-factly, "And you have already wasted ten minutes of your massage. Let's go!"

At least I knew who I was dealing with. Once in the massage chamber, Sergey had me lie down on an uncomfortable metal table that looked like the perfect place to perform autopsies. He tried to remove my apron quickly, but it would not pull away, as my cock was secured in the pocket again and the apron had gotten knotted up during my hijinks with Domo Thisass.

Because the loudspeaker had not allowed me to complete my mission with Domo, my cock, though not hard, was still half hard and near bursting. Sergey extracted my cock from the apron hole with a tsk and removed the apron. He looked at my manhood a bit too long, perhaps with admiration, or perhaps with indifference, and said something under his breath in Hungarian.

He then proceeded to hose me down with warm water and then used soap to lather me up. He was speedy and not very intimate, at first. But whenever his fingers would touch my balls, my cock would get a little bit more erect. Eventually it snaked its way up my belly, almost reaching my chest and rising off my navel. He tsked-tsked again but I could tell he was mesmerized by it. When the massage began in earnest, he would slap the oil on me almost as if he resented having to do it. Splat on my chest, then rub, rub, rub. Splat on my stomach and cock, rub, rub, rub.

I noticed he would invariably rub my shaft just below the head with his forearm while seeming to massage another part of my body with his hands or fingers. This would drive me to near ecstasy, but then he'd execute a move that would be so hard it hurt. I'd clutch the metal lips of the table, and his groin would on occasion make contact with my hand. His cock was hard. I was sure of it.

He instructed me to flip over, and I dutifully complied. It was uncomfortable lying on my hard cock, so I fed it down between my legs as best I could. Sergey stretched my legs, seeming to take pleasure in any discomfort I experienced. Every toe and knee popped. He then laid atop me pushing his weight into me. He rubbed his hardened cock against my crack. I could feel the stiffness but not the loincloth. When had he removed it? Then, he flipped around like an acrobat and sat atop my cheeks. He pulled each leg back toward his crotch until my toes felt balls.

For his next move he kneeled on my cheeks and with amazing muscle control let his thighs ever so slowly slide down either side of my ass. This had me nervous, as my ass checks spread and I felt his hard cock against my hole. But soon he stood on the table straddling me and pulled each leg, one-by-one, up past his cock until my foot was touching his chest, he then pulled me up with straps until my back cracked twice.

Then, he hopped off the table and moved to my head, pressing his still-erect cock against my hair and started doing this finger motion on my neck, like a giant tarantula with slick, rounded feet. Surprisingly, this motion released tension I didn't even know I had. I started to doze off, feeling the weight of jetlag, when I suddenly felt his cock rubbing against my hair followed by a shudder and gasp from him, and a warm trickle down my neck.

When this happened, he muttered something like, "ew-x-a-te." It didn't exactly sound like the Hungarian I'd been hearing so far that day, and it was definitely not Russian. If I had to guess, I'd say Latin – but that would be ridiculous. It probably meant fuck yeah in Hungarian.

He then rubbed his cum into my hair, dare I say, almost lovingly with his fingers. Then he rinsed me off and even used shampoo. This time as he sprayed me down, I spied a tattoo on his left hand. It was like Mihol's. It was hard to make out, but I believe it read HO. I grabbed his hand, which he was not expecting.

"What's this? This tattoo?" I queried a little harsher than I had meant.

"It is nothing," he said. "A friend's initials. He died."

Now I felt horrible. I dropped his hand and said, "I'm sorry for your loss."

"Like I said, it is nothing," he said rather nonchalantly. "It was a long time ago. Now we are closing, and I must bid you adieux. My colleague brought you your clothes from your locker and a towel."

It was then I noticed the key was no longer on my wrist. I remember now he removed it as he was massaging my arm. I grabbed my clothes and frantically searched them.

"Do not worry. It is all there," he responded. "We would not stay in business if we stole the tourists' money. I wasn't thinking about my money. I was thinking about my phone and glasses but both were there. I breathed a sigh of relief. Then I noticed the phone was off. I never turn my phone off.

Chapter 11

I dressed, turned my phone back on, donned my glasses, and gave Sergey a hug and a kiss on each cheek. After all we had had some kind of moment. Hadn't we? I then walked out of the bath and was enveloped by the night.

Heading back on foot toward my hotel but not quite ready for bed yet. It was still early, and I was still horny. I decided to take in more local culture and I took a detour away from the river towards the old Jewish quarter of the city.

My destination was a romkocsma, or ruin bar, that Zitson told me about. This one was a club popular with gays and had been created in a hollowed-out portion of an old factory. It was awesome and spooky at the same time. One thing was for sure; it would never pass building inspection back in the States. It was decorated not just with old cars, but with large chunks of wrecked cars, the kind that you had to cut out the survivors with the jaws of life. There were tires and hubcaps hanging everywhere. Around the dance floor, rusting gas pumps leaned on each other, their hoses loose and lewd, everything catawampus, splashed with neon paint, and lit with black light only, as if a dreadful accident had happened during a Mardi Gras parade.

Shortly after I arrived, I saddled up to the bar (the bar stools were steering wheels) and ordered a beer in Russian, which earned me a strained look from the barkeep. The bar was far from packed, it was a weeknight after all, but the folks that were there were pretty rowdy. Despite it being midweek, there was entertainment.

Instead of a drag queen, which is what I might expect to see in a bar in DC on a weeknight, there was a young waif of a guy, naked, save for a towel wrapped around his waist, dancing on the bar. Zitson warned me to watch out for prostitutes, who might approach promising companionship and only later demanding money. Alas, no one approached me, at first. Eventually, however, towel boy did. He could not have been much older than 20. He started dancing over my beer on the bar and then lowered himself so that my hands, currently wrapped around the base of my beer, rubbed up against his cock.

This is how I knew he was naked except for the towel. He kept moving slightly up and down getting hard. "What's your name?" He asked in English. "I'm Horace Huang," I said. "Yours?" I asked.

"Ryder Ovkok." He replied, nonchalantly. "I'm pleased to meet you." He said as he momentarily looked away and then back at me, deep into my eyes.

He may have been young, but oddly I sensed he was an old soul. I have no idea why I thought that; it was just a feeling. "Don't look now, but there are two Hungarian guys who came in right after you and haven't stopped checking you out since you got here and I don't mean checking you out in a sexual way. Were you followed?"

Fuck! I thought. I hadn't even noticed. "Probably," I answered in equal nonchalance. I then took a drink of my beer, after I played with his hardening cock. I quietly said my glasses prompt and the word, "rearview," which allowed me to zero in on two brutish looking guys who stared at my back.

As quietly as I had spoken, Ryder must have heard me, because he said, "Anything for you Mr. Huang." He stood up, turned around and dropping down and putting the towel over my head so that my face was up against his sweet ass. It smelled of whisky and cigar smoke, in other words delicious. I couldn't see the crowd, but I heard them cheer. I gave a quick lick and felt him shudder. He then stood up, turned around, crouched down, and gave me a peck on my right cheek.

"Thank you for being a good sport," he said loudly in English. Then, more quietly to me, he said, "I must put on a show. I suggest you make your exit while I distract."

He stood up, and without using his hands, he pulled my beer bottle out of mine using only his butt cheeks. As he gracefully moved down the top of the bar expertly avoiding the clientele's drinks, I noticed something akin to a tail protruding out from under his short towel. He removed the beer bottle from his behind and gallantly hopped off the bar and made his way to the two Hungarians.

He drained what was left of the beer on his way and gave a loud belch. He then started his show. He gave the beer bottle a mock blow job, leaving its neck covered in spittle. When he was done he handed the empty, dripping bottle to one of the two guys who looked perplexed.

He guided the bottle to a height just below his own waist and placed it at a 45-degree angle. He removed his towel and put it over the other Hungarian tail's shoulder while grabbing his hands, Ryder then bent over slightly and proceeded to back on to the bottle, inserting it into his rectum. The small crowd erupted in cheers as he began to ride the bottleneck faster and faster and faster.

The two Hungarians were so taken with the sex act that had been thrust upon them that they didn't notice me as I slipped out of the bar. A part of me wanted to take them out, but Johnson's words were always in the back of my mind. You need to blend into the background, *never*, ever make a scene, he had said. On this note I slipped down the darkest streets making my way back to the hotel using the gizmo's map-guidance system.

I did not relax until I was safely sequestered in my room. Immediately upon my return I connected my phone to my laptop and initiated a scan using the Agency's software. We're supposed to do this at least once a day when working in the field. I would have totally blown it off if I didn't have a sneaking suspicion.

My understanding of how it worked is it connected the phone to a ghost-server to see if any malware was installed and whether the phone was tampered with. After 15 minutes or so, it came back as negative for most malware, however it did come back positive for GPS tracking software. This had not been there the day before. That wasn't too bad. Then the laptop screen popped up with a message saying a clone of the phone was made today.

Suddenly, I was grateful for the lovely Agency requirement of a no-use-of-an-Agency-phone-for-personal-reasons policy. Say what one will about the bureaucracy of the Agency, when one goes into the field, he is issued a phone with a complete back story for one's trip already installed. The only thing questionable on this phone was the software that ran the gizmos, which were surely encrypted, and the pictures I took at the restaurant before I went to the bath. No criminal is going to connect the people at that dinner to this investigation. They won't even know about the Agency as there would be no mention of it on the phone.

I wouldn't be surprised if the Agency didn't have a little surprise for the criminal enterprise that was attempting to penetrate their system even now. This thought was interrupted by a knock at my door. I shuddered. I wasn't expecting anyone.

Chapter 12

I looked through the peephole and saw the driver, Yuri.

"Good evening, sir. I have your room service order," he said, as I opened the door.

"But I didn't order room service," I replied.

"Pity," he said. "Well, I would hate for all this to go to waste. This said, we are never allowed to go into a guest room unless we are asked." He was carrying a silver tray with two Heinekens and a silver dish of mixed nuts. He looked at me patiently.

Once I realized what he was implying, it took me a minute, I smiled, and said, "Well in that case, please come in."

Once inside, he said, "I mean, we are never to come into a guest's room unless we are a maid or room service."

"Do you ever work room service?" I asked.

"When the kitchen is short-staffed, and technically it's closed right now, so they are very short-staffed," he stated matter-of-factly.

"I wish to apologize for earlier. The guests I was driving when you called me asked me to take them to dinner. When we arrived at the restaurant, the younger gentleman said he wouldn't be dining tonight and that he needed me to take him somewhere else. I explained that

I was expected back at the hotel. Then he handed me 40,000 Forint. That was a lot of money, so I drove him, no questions asked."

"Where did he need you to take him?" I asked, trying to say it as nonchalantly as possible.

"Some shop on the other side of the city," He replied. "Then I had to wait for over an hour for him."

"What kind of shop was it?" I asked trying to act concerned for Yuri.

"Look, Mister, supposedly-a-pharmaceutical-sales guy from Wisconsin who happens to speak fluent Russian. What is it to you? And should I add, he's a far better tipper than you. Are you a spy?" He lobbed the question as if to ask me if I took cream in my coffee, so I answered in kind.

"Not exactly," I said with a studied shrug. "Don't let looks fool you, I *am* an American, I just wasn't born there. I spent most of my childhood in Việt Nam. I went to a Russian school until Glasnost, and once relations improved with the U. S, an American school, and on to high school in Wisconsin. Wanna see my transcripts?"

I grinned and he relaxed. He then removed the caps off the two beers and handed me one. "So, not exactly a spy?" he queried as we clinked our bottles together.

"The two men you drove earlier, they work for a rival pharmaceutical company," I took a sip of the beer hoping I'd put one over on him. No such luck.

"You are a bad liar," he said. "Look, the professor comes here often. He works for a UN agency. They are staying in the presidential suites. What's your interest in them?" he asked pointedly. "Or should I tell them of your interest?"

"No. no, no," I said. "I work for the same agency as the professor, and every Agency employee, no matter who they are, must adhere to spending guidelines, yet these two don't. First class airfare, finest suites at the finest hotels, and the finest restaurants. It doesn't add up. So, I was asked to investigate them. That's all."

"Because he is very high up in your agency, they treat him well," Yuri countered, "I don't see the problem."

"Look," I said, "even the head of the Agency, the professor's boss's boss doesn't get this kind of treatment. So, I'm here looking into it. Just making sure everything is on the up and up."

Yuri got a wicked grin on his face and said, "So then you are a sexy spy. I would not betray you, even if they ripped off my clothes and tortured me." He said this as he fondled his cock.

It was then that I threw a pillow from the couch at him, and he burst out laughing in the most adorable way.

"Oh, come here," he reached out to me with his massive arms and pulled me up against his washboard abs and stiffening endowment. "I would never betray you. I will help you."

"Why would you help me? I pondered.

"Because you're right. It doesn't make sense. And you are a super sexy spy."

"I'm just an analyst," I retorted. "But, if this goes well, it could make my career.

"Well," Yuri said. "I'd like to make you."

Just then his tongue slipped into my mouth. I already was with two other guys that night; well, three if you count towel boy. While two came on me, they all left me, well... hanging. Who gets a massage where the masseur gets off and the client doesn't? Yuri unbuttoned my shirt, and I returned the favor. He teased my left nipple, which is the sensitive one. When he heard me gasp a little, he started sucking on it flicking his tongue back and forth across it and softly biting it.

He dropped to my crotch and nuzzled my ever-hardening cock. He stripped off my pants and underwear and paused to admire my cock, looking up at me and smiling before he started playing with it, slapping it against his cheeks, then sucking on the head.

Soon we moved to the bed and settled into a 69. He had a nice cock himself, and I started darting my tongue between his dick, balls, taint, and hole, until finally I went to town on his tight hole, which made him moan over and over. My cock was so hard I worried not enough blood was going to my brain. A good spy needs stamina to fuel his hard cock, but also his hardy mind.

After a while, he lay alongside me, his hard dick pressed into my side. It was then that he asked me in Russian, "May I fuck you?"

I responded in Russian, "Nyet. But I can fuck you."

"Nyet," he said, "I am what you Americans call a 100% certified top."

"You didn't seem like a top when I had my tongue in your hole," I countered.

"I like my ass to be eaten, but that's as far as I go with the butt-stuff," he said in English as he faced me.

I began to crack up, "We don't usually say butt-stuff in English," I said. "But...I get your point. Why don't you have a nice seat on my chin? And I will clean your kitchen."

"What?" he said, confused.

I pointed to his hole and then to my mouth and then said, "I love to eat ass and I am a 100% certified top too. My favorite thing to do sexually, next to topping is, eating ass and I can do it for hours, literally."

He responded by mounting my face faster than a rodeo hooker on payday.

We finished around 3:00 a.m. Time does fly when you're having sex. He came twice all over me. I just came once, but it was fucking amazing. We took a shower together and collapsed in the bed.

During pillow talk I asked him, "Answer me this, we took a side trip this afternoon, after you collected me, so how did their luggage get to the hotel before we did?"

He took a swig of his beer, which was on the bedside table, then said, "They probably shipped it ahead to avoid the hassle. Lots of rich people do that," he said.

"My point exactly," I said. "The Agency doesn't pay for that."

"Maybe the professor is rich."

"No, my investigation hasn't uncovered anything like that." I said as I pondered. Eventually, I drifted off.

My alarm went off at 7:00 a.m. and he was gone. At 7:15 my room phone rang. It was Yuri.

"Mr. Huang, I trust you slept well. This is Yuri in guest services." He said this in a very business-like manner. "Room service has left coffee outside your door. Did you still need transport to the UN Shared Services Center this morning?"

I responded, "Good morning, Yuri. Yes, I slept very well, I had this amazing dream of a beautiful man..."

"Yes sir, this is good. But about car service?" he said.

I too adopted his business-like demeanor; he was at work after all. I said, "I'd love nothing more than to get a lift from you. However, can you please take the professor and Mihol and arrange another car for me just in case they have any additional destinations?"

"Absolutely sir, it would be my pleasure. My colleague will be waiting for you at the front entrance of the hotel at 8:30 a.m. sharp.

"Koszi, Yuri," I said, which is thank you in Hungarian. It was one of the few Hungarian words I remembered from Cox's lessons.

"My pleasure, sir. Will there be anything else?" Yuri asked.

"My tongue up your ass later," I replied.

"Always my pleasure. Good day, sir." he said as he ended the call.

Chapter 13

At 8:30 a.m. I was downstairs, and I entered the awaiting town car which took me to the UN Shared Services Center or UN-SSC. I checked in under my fake name. The room was cavernous with towering ceilings. It was clad in light woods, and a large UN flag was draped across the front of it. A title slide of a presentation was up on a large screen below the flag. As I walked into the front of the room, I noticed it was set up like a theater, although each row featured interconnected desks. The desks included each of the countries' names, although they were often spelled in a different way than I was used to seeing them.

An unremarkable woman represented Việt Nam and three people were sitting at the United States desk. I vaguely recognized one of the U.S. representatives, but only tangentially, I could not recall his name or position.

I climbed the levels along the side and went to one of the back desks, which was reserved for non-country representatives, as this was where I was directed to sit.

Once I settled in a vacant chair, I was disturbed by something, but I couldn't place it. Then I realized what it was. To my surprise, the room was dead quiet, even though someone had just approached the podium at the front of the room and appeared to be speaking. I grabbed an earpiece with a coiled wire sheathed in plastic off the desk, opened it, plugged it into the receptacle on the desk, and then placed the other end in my ear.

The language I was greeted with sounded like Chinese. I flipped the dial and heard Russian, French, and then English. I stopped there but assumed there were a few more languages represented. The woman speaking was introducing the Undersecretary, Mihol's boss, but I saw no trace of Mihol. I looked to the wings of the stage, but there was no sign of him there.

I texted Yuri. "Are you with Mihol?" I typed.

Soon a reply came through. "Yes. On another errand."

'Where now?' I typed.

"A high-end jewelry store," came the response. Then another message. 'Again, I'm waiting here." This was followed by, "Here he is. I have to go."

A sex shop, a print shop, a tailor, and now a jeweler. Someone getting married? I thought. If the next stop is a bakery, I'll know for certain. I snorted a loud laugh, heads turned, I summoned a fake cough, and I grabbed some water from the pitcher on my desk and poured it into a glass.

Forty-five minutes later, I spied Mihol coming in the back of the room directly across from me. Mihol didn't know me or what I looked like, but I still held my folio up in an effort to block my face, just in case. The Undersecretary was just finishing and now taking questions.

When the Undersecretary finished, there was rapturous applause. A few people left the room, but most stayed. Apparently, in between speakers there was an informal break, as it was not on the schedule.

People got up, some moved around the room, and almost everyone started chatting.

The guy sitting next to me introduced himself and said, "Bonjour. Parlez vous français?

I did, but replied, "No, I do not." This matched my cover story. "Just English." I lied.

In very proper English with only a slight French accent he said, "I am Maxwell Schlong. I work in medical devices. You?"

"Horace Huang. But you can call me, Hor. I work in pharmaceuticals."

"Interesting," he said. He looked down to my crotch, stared for a moment, his eyes lifted to mine and he smiled and said in a friendly way, "Please call me Max." He then asked, have you attended one of these sessions before?"

"No. This is my first time," I said.

"May I ask why your company sent you?" he asked.

This question and the appropriate answer had also been drilled into me back in DC. "Just trying to keep up on the committee 's discussions." Though my answer was practiced, I thought it was a rather nosy question. "And you? Why are you here?" I retorted.

"Same as you, but we also advocate to attendees to help them better understand our products and the treaty exceptions we need. Some of us are meeting with the BRIC group this afternoon for lunch. If you're interested in attending..." He oddly fingered his lips as he said, "It's a free lunch. Anyway, you can see first-hand, how we operate, I mean advocate."

"Thanks, but I have lunch plans," I lied again.

"C'est la vie," he said, then quickly added, "If anything changes, please let me know. I'd love to bring you into the fold." The next speaker was about to begin, so we abruptly ended our conversation.

As the speaker talked, I noticed the same small tattoo on Schlong's left hand as Sergay from last night had. Sergay said it was the initials of a dear friend. Either this was a very popular dear dead friend to countless people who coincidentally happened to be in Budapest currently, or something else was up.

There was a break scheduled after the speaker. So, when he concluded, I turned towards Max Schlong, and feigning indifference asked, "What an interesting tattoo... is it H-O?" I asked pausing between the letters.

"Oh, it's nothing. Leftover from college. It would be like your American fraternities, but for science. How do you say, nerds? There used to be a small two, but it faded away. H_2O, the most important component for all of life."

I pretended this information meant nothing to me.

"It was nice meeting you, Hor. Perhaps we can rendezvous later," he said. As he stood, Max Schlong adjusted what appeared to be a massive tool inside his pants and walked away with a wink and a swagger.

I went out into the conference center's lobby, which was off the back of the room on a higher level than where I entered. There was an assortment of pastries, juices, teas and, most importantly, coffee. I helped myself to the coffee and made it my mission to look for that tattoo on anyone else.

I also spoke to the Undersecretary, complimenting him on his talk that I had barely paid attention to. "How long will you be in Budapest?" I asked him.

He replied, "Just for the week. We're heading back Sunday."

"Oh, are you traveling with your wife?" I asked innocently.

"For God's sake no. She finds these sessions tedious. Just my assistant."

Out of the corner of my eye, I caught Mihol glaring at me contemptuously. Jesus, I thought, what's up with him? Am I moving into his territory? I took my leave before the Undersecretary could ask any questions of me. It wasn't hard. He was in demand. What I did notice, or should I say didn't notice, was he didn't have the HO tattoo on either hand, which only made me wonder, is it always on the right-hand or is it on the left-hand sometimes? And if so, does that have a significance?

This I answered for myself shortly thereafter. It apparently could be on either. I spied three men with the tattoo during the break. Sometimes it was on the right-hand in one case, and the other two times on the left. The men had nothing in common. One was attractive and fit and set off my gaydar. The other two were older, less attractive and left my gaydar, well, limp. One of the older guys was even wearing Middle Eastern robes. I saddled up to the cute one. It wasn't hard. He seemed to approach me. Hey, I'm only human. I started to chat him up. He was, I learned, from the Bulgarian delegation.

"Hi, I'm Horace, Horace Huang. What's your name?" I queried. My Midwestern charm on full power.

"I am pleased to meet you," he said in somewhat broken English. "I am Ilov Giandik."

"I see you are from Bulgaria," having spied his country's name on his badge, I said, "Do you live in Sofia?" I then asked.

"Yes," he smiled, seemingly pleased I knew a city in his country. As a diplomat it was a fair guess that he was from the capital. And you don't go to Russian school for six years and not learn all the capitals of the former USSR.

"And you?" he asked.

"I'm from the United States."

"I mean, yes, I can see this from your badge. Where in the United States are you from? New York? I have always wanted to visit the Big Apple." This he said with a wink in his voice, as if by using the colloquial term for New York City, he was part of the in-crowd.

"Afraid not," I said. "I'm from Wisconsin—"

"—It's famous for its Cheese." He cut me off.

I returned the favor, "And Bulgaria is famous for its yogurt, correct?" I quickly changed the subject since I couldn't care less about dairy products.

"What do you do in Bulgaria? Are you a scientist?" I asked.

"No." He answered quizzically. "I'm an attorney, but I mostly attend these meetings and take notes," he said.

"Do you work out?" he asked, as he grabbed my bicep approvingly.

"I do. How did you guess?" I asked, as I touched his stomach, it was rock hard. He blanched.

"You Americans are so forward," he said as he looked both ways. I noted that no one was paying any attention to us as I looked around.

"Hey, you grabbed me first." I countered.

"Let me give you my number. Maybe we can meet later," he said as he handed me a business card with an international number scrawled on the back.

"Maybe we can grab a drink tonight?" I asked.

"I can't tonight," he said matter-of-factly.

"What about tomorrow night?" I asked.

"We'll see," he said. "Why did you ask me if I was a scientist earlier?"

"This tattoo on your right hand, HO. I heard it was a group of science n...," I switched tactics, "...it represents a scientific society."

He suddenly looked a little scared and responded. "It is just my sister's initials. She passed away."

"Oh, I'm sorry." I feigned remorse but then asked. "I thought your last name was Giandik. Was her last name different?

"So many questions Horace." He said with resolve and a hand on my shoulder. "You should be careful. All those questions could get you into trouble."

He said this as he clapped my shoulder and walked away.

This was the last thing I remembered.

Chapter 14

After that, I vaguely recall being dizzy and maybe being rushed from the room by people who caught me when I fell. Were they waiting for me? I wondered. Now, I'm naked as the day I was born, strapped to a chair while Yuri, my new friend, and I guess betrayer, was strapped down getting his ass reamed on a table by the Frenchman, Tayl Tapper. I hadn't really paid that much attention to him before, but he was massive, both his person and his cock.

"It's your turn Huang Dong, or whatever the fuck your name is," Ben Overntakit said in his thick Eastern-European accent. "And even if you reconsider joining up, I'm still getting my fuck, in what I hope is your tight-ass-virgin hole. He dragged the chair I was strapped to with me in it over to the other table that appeared to be just made for this purpose. He undid one of my arms and strapped it to the table, then undid the other arm, and forced me up and on the table.

But before he could strap my left arm into the leather straps, he said, "I'm going to fuck you looking you in the eye so I can see your face while I pulverize your hole." I assume that's why he hadn't yet strapped down my legs. That was nearly a fatal mistake for him.

Where did I learn my H-to-H skills? The one thing about spending one's childhood in a Russian school is you don't have American-style physical education classes, or as the American's affectionately call it, P.E. Oh, we got an education all right, and boy was it physical. I found myself thanking Mr. Wang, my kung fu and jiu-jitsu teacher and Comrade Wakacokski, who taught us SAMBO, a Russian style of hand-to-hand combat which drew on fighting styles from across the Soviet Republic.

With my legs and my left arm free, I quickly put Ben in a sleeper-hold. With my right thigh and my left leg, I compressed his windpipe and cutoff his breathing supply. Once he passed out, I pushed him off me and flipped head over heels onto the floor and undid my other arm and the ball gag.

Tapper was so into fucking Yuri that he wasn't even aware of what was happening and that he was my next victim. I had been pretty stealthy, so I gave myself credit. I jumped up on the other table and came up behind him and boxed his ears. This completely disoriented him.

Next, I pulled him up into a chokehold, which wasn't easy given his size. There was a popping noise as his cock exited Yuri's ass. Little did I know Tapper was really close to coming. As I asphyxiated him, he started convulsing and coming at the same time. He started spraying out from his massive cock seemingly gallons and gallons of cum. It sprayed all over Yuri's back and ass. The spasms were violent, yet he was moaning with ecstasy. Once incapacitated, I remembered how some guys like to be choked during orgasm, as it, allegedly and supposedly, intensifies it? That said, I'm sure they aren't going for complete unconsciousness.

I untied and un-gagged Yuri. I found some hot wet towels in a steamer drawer. This is a first-class dungeon, I thought to myself, and handed a couple to Yuri. Since Tayl Tapper and Ben Overntakit were already on the tables, I just needed to rearrange them and strap them down.

"Do you want to take your revenge, Yuri?" I asked. "I can put Tapper ass up."

"I'm tempted. But no," he said. "I'm sorry for telling them about you. Mihol offered me a bigger tip, but I'm pretty sure they were on to you already."

"Bigger than this? I joked pointing to my dick.

"You know what I mean," he said.

"I don't appreciate what you did," I said, suddenly serious. "I liked you a lot but I don't think it's a good idea to stay friends. I'm not going to lecture. I think you got appropriately punished for your deception.

"I hate to admit it." Yuri said. "But I kind of enjoyed it. Thankfully, I always had bondage fantasies, though I think those fantasies are over for now, Hor. Or should I call you Dong?

"Just call me Mr. Huang please," I said more coldly than I meant. I was still pretty pissed off. If it hadn't been for my teachers Wang and Wakacokski who knew what shape my beloved rosebud would be in right now. There was no point in ruminating. I pointed to the closet and asked,

"Are your clothes in there?"

"Yes," Yuri said.

I went to the closet and pulled his clothes out which were next to mine. As I did so, I noticed an abandoned garment bag on the floor. I also noticed my phone was in my jacket pocket. I handed his clothes to him and started putting mine in the garment bag.

Aren't you getting dressed? he asked.

"No," I said. "I have the element of surprise and I'm going to see what the fuck is going on here. As I said earlier, I'm on an investigation." Then added. "Why are you naked?"

"They convinced me to be strapped down and naked in a chair so you wouldn't know, well, you know..." he trailed off.

"And you fell for that?"

"Yes, I stupidly did," he said, contritely.

I started poking around the room. Azramar's suit hung in the closet and the spit-bloodied shirt was crumpled on the floor. As I continued looking around in all the cupboards and closets, I saw a pair of gleaming tools. Machines, really. Two metal boxes with long rods and pistons, specifically. Best of all, each had a dildo on the end of each rod. I knew exactly what they were, given the hours I had dedicated to watching porn.

"Help me with these," I commanded Yuri.

"What are they?" he asked.

"Fuck machines." I said.

We each set one up on each of the tables currently holding the unconscious Big-Dicked guys.

The table had electrical outlets built in, seemingly designed for just such an occasion. The machines even locked into the tables. The tables had tie-downs at various spots. I repositioned Ben Overntakit while Yuri repositioned Tayl Tapper. We took extra care to keep them anchored down at all times.

"Should we lube them up?" Yuri asked.

"Did he use lube on you?" I retorted.

"A little!" Yuri said angrily.

"Then I guess we give them just a little." I said.

We got the machines perfectly aligned with our assailants' holes. We each went over to the large barrel of lube in the corner with the handpump and dispensed just enough lube, but not too much, to lube the dildo. Yuri then got dressed and I grabbed one of the warm, wet, hot towels from the drawer and put it over my shoulder. Azramar left naked so I assumed I'd attract less attention naked as well. I found a pen attached to a cleaning clipboard, of all things, and scrawled the letters HO on my left hand.

"Aren't you going to wrap that around your waist?" Yuri asked pointing to the towel.

"No," I responded. "Again, you're getting out of here. I'm getting to the bottom of this. I want you to go to the hotel and pack up all my things. That place is no longer safe for me. Be back here in 90 minutes with one of the hotel cars; I'll need a lift. You owe me this much. Don't forget my passport. Where are we anyway?" Despite being connected to a satellite, my spyglasses weren't great when it came to subterranean unmapped territory.

"We're somewhere close to the Rudas Bath. Do you know it?" Yuri said.

"I figured as much." I replied, having been suspicious of it since my phone had been tampered with when I visited it just last night. "You could say yes, I know it intimately."

We then left the room, and not before turning on the fuck machines. Ben Overntakit and Tayl Tapper came to instantly and started screaming. What babies! I guess some rapists just can't enjoy getting ass-raped themselves, even with a little lube. They're fine dishing it out, but they just can't take it.

I turned at the door to take a last look as they had suddenly fallen quiet. The fuck machines were still moving in and out like pistons. I guess the attached dildos hit their prostrates simultaneously because they had both stopped screaming at the same time and now were moaning. Was it in ecstasy? Maybe.

We locked the door from the inside before we shut it. Yuri found an "In Use. Do Not Disturb" sign on the ground which he hung on the doorknob. We wished each other luck and parted ways, each of us heading in opposite directions.

Chapter 15

I moved down the cave-like tunnel with the towel over my left shoulder and the garment bag slung over my right. I was prepared to fight when I encountered others, all men of course, and of all different nationalities, but no alarm was made in response to my presence. Everyone was naked. Typically, they just looked at my cock. As I had not turned off the facial recognition software on my glasses, the software kept reporting names to me, but no intel stuck out as important.

Though I looked at each guy in the face, I'm confident none could pick me out of a police lineup, at least a standard one where the perps were wearing clothes.

I did duck into a side tunnel twice, when I heard footsteps approach because for all I knew, Azramar could be my next encounter. However, when I heard the next footsteps there was no such hiding place. The two naked guys greeted me with, "Ci ya," a Hungarian form of hello. Yeah, another word I remembered from my lessons. I passed a shower room cleaved out of stone, a space with a sunken pit lined with a circular couch, then another dungeon-like room, this one with the door open.

One guy was in the sling, while the other was having his way on his ass. The man in the sling was taunting, “Harder! Is that all ya got?” I’m pretty sure that’s what he was saying, although it was in Hungarian. It had a gritted teeth, guttural cadence.

I circled back to the couch room and stashed the garment bag, leaving my phone in it. This place was carved out of rock and there was a mild sulfuric smell. It was either very near the natural hot springs of the bath, or a portal to hell. At this point, a total toss-up. I then reached an opening in the wall that looked down on an immense cavern. It’s difficult to describe, but it resembled a set from an Indiana Jones movie. Men were milling around, mostly naked, though many wore somewhat translucent robes. There were ledges at various heights with drums on them.

A large black man seemed to test out his drum. “Thwap, Thwap, Thwap,” went the report. On closer inspection, I noticed he literally slapped his giant dick against the drum skin.

Then I heard a familiar voice come down the hall.

Azramar!

This time I ducked into an adjacent anti-chamber and peeked out. It was him and he was joined by none other than Phillip Mihol. They stopped at the opening I just looked out of.

“See it is perfect. And just at the point of consummation, the full moon will pass through the aperture in the ceiling,” said Azramar. “But you must maintain the sex for 47 minutes. You’ll know when the moon has passed across the aperture and then you must time your orgasms to be simultaneous.”

"Look, Manuel," Phillip said. "I can do that, but you've yet to find someone who can keep pace and don't get me started on the inadequacy of some of your past prospects."

"Not to worry my sweetest ass...asset," he said while he played with Mihol's beautiful ass.

I don't know why, but this enraged me.

"Even now he's prepping himself in the steam room," Azramar said.

"Does that help?" Mihol asked.

Azramar replied, "I think he's in there getting the wrinkles out of his robes. It was a long trip from Singapore."

"Singapore? Hasn't he ever heard of a drycleaner?" Mihol said.

"Well, these robes are unusual." Azramar said with a bit of sarcasm in his voice. "You can't just take them to the fluff and fold without sparking a query or two. Our man in Singapore has assured me he is big, big, big and has the staying power of a freight train through tundra, no brakes no mercy. What about you? Are your robes, jewels, and accouterments ready?"

"Yes, because I had the sense to source them here," said Mihol.

"¡Perfecto!" Azramar proclaimed. "Showtime in one hour. Get to your attendants and prepare yourself."

"For the record," Mihol started. "I have no expectations for this evening."

"Well, then perhaps you will be pleasantly surprised," retorted Azramar.

After I was sure they were gone, I made my way back to the showers I passed on my way back here, in hopes that's where the steam room was located. Sure enough, I found it. I wrapped the towel around my waist and entered. Inside I found an anxiety-ridden and well-hung, Asian man who paced back and forth. His dick was certainly above average, but needless to say, still no competition. As my phone was within proximity, my glasses reported to me that his name was Peter Inurbutt from Singapore.

He immediately broke the #1 cardinal rule of the gay steam room: "no talking" and said "Are you one of the attendants? I thought I had another hour and a half."

"You have one hour," I said. I then adopted a friendly attitude and said, "Hello. I'm Hor. What's your name?"

He marshaled all his bluster and said, "I am the Kong Dong."

I started laughing and said just one word, "Seriously."

Surprisingly, he laughed too. "That's what I said to Remy back home. Sorry. My name is Peter. You said your name is Hor?"

"Yea, it's short for Horace." I then asked, "Who's Remy?"

"He's this guy I hooked up with back home. I was saying I wanted to travel and that I really wanted to visit Europe. So, he cooked up the scheme and here I am. Supposedly I'm going to have to fuck this hot white guy in front of an audience. It sounded like a good idea back in Singapore, like I won the 4D. In addition, they're going to pay me all this money. I'll be able to head back home after I've had my fill of Europe and get the 5C's.

I didn't know what the hell he meant by the 4D and the 5Cs, but my glasses did.

They reported to me that in Singapore the 4D is a lottery operated by the government-owned Singapore Pools, while the 5Cs stand for cash, car, credit card, condominium, and country club. Which added up to 7Cs, but I ignored this and just said, "And now here you are. Mission accomplished."

"Yeah, except for the public fucking part," he said with a grimace.

"It beats a public flogging," I quipped. Singapore is still infamous for meting out public canings to scofflaws for the most minor of offenses.

"I'm more of a one-on-one kind of guy, if you know what I mean," he said. "To top it all off, my Viagra got seized at the airport. Though, as a consolation, the border agent was hot," he added.

This immediately made me think of Domo Thisass and his sweet hole from last night. I pushed those thoughts away and said "Boy, it's hot in here," I said this as I removed my towel and wiped my brow with it. My action had the desired effect.

He screamed, "You're fucking huge! I have never seen a dick that big. You're the Kong Dong, not me."

"Moi? Whatever do you mean?" I asked with false modesty.

"Look at you," he stammered.

"I've seen me before. I don't need to look."

"You need to take my place," he pleaded.

"I think they'd notice," I said.

"No, to them we all look alike. Besides, there's this mask. Well, helmet really. Here, try it on," he said as he handed this ancient looking horned contraption to me.

I lowered it onto my head. It was heavy and I could barely see out of it though it accommodated my glasses perfectly. "How are you supposed to see with this thing on?" I asked. Too bad my glasses didn't have that Xray feature Johnson had joked about. Though I did note that despite the humidity in the room they had not steamed up.

"That's why there are at least four attendants. They guide you and your cock into the hole, like horse breeders. Plus, I was promised once up close for the sex part, you can see through this mouth hole." Peter said while pointing at the mouthpiece. He was right. I could see his finger and him. He said all this with pleading in his voice.

I feigned indifference saying, "It won't work. We do not look similar enough."

Inurbutt kept pleading. Finally, he said, "Look, it's settled. You are much more of a Kong Dong than me. Now let me run you through the details."

I pretended to accept reluctantly, which of course had been my plan all along. I was just glad that he made it easy and I didn't have to waylay him. Twelve minutes later, I had the lay of the land and most of the expectations of the evening. All I knew was that Mihol was the star of the show, and he was my target. After all, I was under specific instructions from my boss, an official of a UN Agency, to nail him.

It all made sense now. Who was paying for all the upgrades, restaurants and everything else. Azramar or his henchmen. I was finally going to get to the bottom of Phillip Mihol and his secrets. After this conclusion, Peter Inurbutt and I agreed he should make himself scarce, and then slip out once the festivities began.

Chapter 16

Before the attendants arrived, I found a protein shake in the lounge-like area adjacent to the shower, where I earlier stowed my bag behind a sofa. I downed the shake and some fruit and cheese that was in a bowl on a table.

I was starving. I had already donned the full wrinkle-free outfit, which surprisingly was not that revealing. It came with gold-colored bangle bracelets, which conveniently covered my watch, and a belt. There was a loin cloth that was attached to the belt with Velcro and could be torn off for the BIG reveal. I kept my back to the entry and the helmet ready at my side so that I could put it on the minute anyone approached. When no one was around I peeked out into the corridor.

When I looked back towards the lounge, I saw a sign I missed earlier. It was in Latin, but under the Latin it read in English, "Kong Dong Lounge." Well, at least I was making use of my own quarters, I thought.

I didn't know if Inurbutt met any of the attendants before. So, when I heard an adjacent door open and footsteps, I put the helmet on and said to the first man within earshot, "If I act strange it is because I am getting in the zone." Whatever the hell that meant. It didn't matter; he bought it.

The attendants were super respectful. They referred to me as Glorious-Kong-Dong or Oh-Most Venerable-Kong-Dong, one even said He-Whose-Massive-Mast-I-Wish-To-Sit-Atop. All I thought was, I could get used to this. They all had the HO tattoo on their right-hands signifying they were of the power-bottom persuasion.

While one of the attendants addressed a strap on my inner thigh, I heard an audible gasp when he seemed to accidentally bump up against my tool. I heard him express something. I think it was in Tagalog, though they had all been speaking fluent English up until that point. Shortly after the accidental bump, each attendant began to carefully check both sides of the thigh straps. My cock stirred at all the furtive attention.

It was then that Azramar came in. I recognized his voice immediately when he said, "You ready Kong Dong?"

I grunted in reply.

"You were a little more animated earlier," Azramar remarked.

Azramar stood back and looked at me. Something looked amiss. He stepped closer and peered through my mouth hole. All he got back was reflection from my glasses. He groaned in disappointment. My balls shrank into their sockets when he reached up and touched the mask, my breath left for greener pastures.

He will pull the mask off and kill me, my balls shouted from their hidey holes. I prepared myself to lay him out cold. Instead, Azramar licked his thumb and rubbed off a smudge as if he just detailed a luxury car and noticed a missed spot. I needed to look immaculate to fuck some sex slave in the ass? I took a deep breath. This must be some big deal.

“Fair enough,” Azramar said and my balls dropped like a bull about to mount a heifer. “Well, the Ass...I mean the Asset, will be prepared. Normally all his attendants would fuck him in preparation for you, but tonight they’ll each have a crystal dildo of a different size, and they’ll work their way up to just under your size.

Once that is done the chanting will start and that’s when the boys here will bring you down to him. Until then, just stand there looking fierce. Kind of like you are doing now. ¡Dios mío! You are scaring the shit out of me, Kong Dong.”

He started to walk past me, but then instead turned toward me and said, “He’s decked out in jewels. Try not to displace any of them. They’re on loan and worth a fortune. They’ll sparkle almost magically in the moonlight. Everything is perfect, so don’t fuck this up, Kong Dong. He then passed me, shook his head, or at least appeared to from my poor vantage, and took his leave.

The attendants helped me downstairs. They asked if I wanted to take the helmet off until show time, but I declined. Soon we were at one of the lower entrances to the cavern I saw earlier from above.

The cavern was lit with both torches and electric lights inter-mixed. The cavern looked bigger from below than it had looked earlier from above. There were also now more guys on the small ledges beating on drums. Some were masked, some were not, all were naked. The drums were at least beating in rhythm. I couldn’t see if the one guy was still beating the drum with his cock, though I tried. I did see lots of other naked men, some standing around, pleasuring themselves and a few pleasuring one another, all had a small mark on one of their hands or the other. I’m sure they all read HO.

All focus was on the middle of the room where beautiful Phillip Mihol, clad in a black robe with slits on the sides exposing his muscular thighs, was reclining on black silk sheets. I did catch the sparkle of jewels, apparently reflecting the light of torches as the moon was not yet visible in the aperture overhead.

Phillip rolled over and lay on his stomach. The robe was lifted up by one of his attendants, and he backed up onto his haunches. If I positioned my head just right, I had a perfect view through the mouth hole of the most beautiful ass I ever beheld. Was it better than the one in my dream the other week? I think so.

Three naked men knelt on each side of him. One by one, they took turns shoving crystal dildos up his ass, first slowly, and then they sped up. They'd slap his ass on occasion, but they always kept up the rhythm to the beats of the drum, which seemed to be going faster and faster. With each slap or new dildo, Mihol arched his back almost theatrically. One of the guys shoved his cock in Mihol's mouth. My cock responded instantly, and I grew angry, again. Dildos were one thing, but the cock was flesh.

I saw more than one person pointing at my erection under my robe. Through the aperture above came the first hint of moonlight, but you could not yet see the moon. When the first sliver of moonlight showed, the drumming stopped and Azramar came forward near the sunken bedding in the center, but he did not stand on it.

"Brethren," he cried out. "For more than 2,000 years, we gathered to mark the passing of the seasons. Tonight, is the first full moon after the autumnal equinox. Thank you for attending these festivities. Just as the moon silently wields its power over our world, it shapes the tides, so too do we exert quiet influence across the globe. The moon stabilizes our world; similarly, Homosexus Obsessi is a stabilizing force on this planet. May Homosexus Obsessi forever reign supreme. Nothing significant happens on this Earth without our hand in it. Together, we watch out for one another, as we have for millennia. We sustain our members carnally and financially. We never discriminate against any man regardless of race, creed, or station in life."

It was not lost on me that while any gay man could probably join if he had the right asset, he was slightly discriminating against roughly 50% of the human population who could never join. And, well straight men were a bit counted out as well, so make that 95%.

As he continued blathering, I was losing my hard-on.

"Any man can join our group if judged worthy by one of you or any other member. If he is not endowed with an exemplary appendage, he can always offer up his ass as long as he can take a giant cock and take it well," he said. I had a pretty good view of him, so I noticed at this point, he grabbed his own half-hard cock and started stroking it. "He can be anointed, as long as he agrees to these terms and our very good way of life. So now fellow members, for the main event. We have scoured many lands and brought the largest cock holder to help satiate our most prized and willing ass, or eh, asset. Oh, great and venerated Kong Dong, will you take our most humble and willing servant and plunder him?

I grunted. It seemed appropriate.

"Here he lay willing and prepared before you. Attendants, prepare the Kong Dong!"

Azramar walked away and took a seat close to the action. The Filipino attendants pulled my robes off, and yanked my loin cloth away, brushing ever so slightly against my stomach, which immediately started stiffening my rod. I was left clad only with the helmet, the bangles, and the belt. The assembled crowd gasped. The attendants then proceeded to pull, tug, lick and suck my giant tool and play with my cheeks. A tongue entered my hole teasingly.

The drums started up again and those assembled yelled out repeatedly, "Kong Dong! Kong Dong! Kong Dong!"

I was enjoying this action and was imagining Phillip Mihol gasping with desire. But when I looked down, his back was still turned towards me with the beautiful cheeks spread. The room was in a frenzy and so was my cock, which was raging hard. The attendants guided me down to Mihol. One of the attendants lined up my cock with Mihol's puckering hole. Feeling like a prize stallion, I thrust. Mihol arched his back and whinnied. Just at that moment I looked up through the ceiling. The silver lining of the moon had just become visible. So, I thrust to the shouts of Kong Dong, and the beat of the drums.

"All hail the Kong Dong! All hail the Kong Dong! Fuck him Kong Dong! Fuck him!!!" The crowd roared.

My cock had slipped in fully and with no resistance. It fit like a glove. In all my life, I never found an asshole or a throat that could take it all, but here is the one I searched for all my life. I fucked him and I fucked him. I wanted to take him every which way, but the helmet made that difficult. I got on my feet and drove my cock in repeatedly, my thighs were on the side of his hips, my hands clasped his shoulders, and my cock buried in him to the hilt. In and out, in and out I thrust.

When I stopped to take a breath or two, Mihol, with my cock still deep inside him, twisted over to face me. He played with my nipples and my balls. I put his legs over my shoulders and repeatedly buried my shaft deep within him. Fucking his hole. It felt so good. I then pulled his right leg over to join his left leg on my left shoulder, while I continued to ride his ass hard.

At one point, I think he stared in my helmet's eye sockets. I pinned down his arms, and just laid into his sweet, sweet ass. I then pulled one of his legs down and threaded it through my legs and pushed his other leg straight up. It ran along my stomach, chest and my shoulder. I looked up and saw the moon filling the aperture. This made me fuck him harder. His legs scissored me as I took in the moon.

I fucked on and Mihol kept up with me at every thrust. Truly, where had he been all my life? To think, for the last four years, he worked mere floors above me. I could have partook of this ass all this time! This just made me fuck him harder. I couldn't believe anyone could take this. But he matched me thrust by thrust, me and my massive donkey schlong.

Unbeknownst to me, while this continued, I learned one of Azramar's colleagues approached him somewhere in the middle of the melee. I later could only imagine the exchange.

"Master Azramar," the colleague likely said. "We just found Ben Overntakit and Tayl Tapper tied down in dungeon one, being fucked without mercy."

"By whom?" Azramar would ask in his attempt at proper English.

"The fuck machines that were in the storage closet."

"That is unfortunate. Where are the prisoners?"

"We found the Judas on the security feed, leaving the compound."

"And Dong?" Azramar's blood pressure would dangerously rise right about now.

"We have no idea, sir, but there's something else. We also found Peter Inurbutt left the complex about a half-hour later, through the same exit as the traitor."

"Well, if Inurbutt left, then who is that?" He would've then pointed directly at me, while I happily blasted away at Mihol's insatiable hole.

The Moon's final sliver was evident through the aperture. I lay on my back and Mihol was sitting atop me, bouncing up and down on my cock from tip to base, seemingly effortlessly. My cock had never come out during our entire lovemaking session.

"We're supposed to come now," I said through gasps of air.

"I can't stop," Mihol said.

"It's time for my moon-shot," I said. "Oh my God, I'm coming."

Phillip hopped off of me and I hosed his face fireman-style. My second blast hit his chest. And the third blast? Well, he was rubbing his hard cock against mine and it was covered in my semen. The fourth blast, usually unheard of for me, hit him in his open mouth. He wiped the cum from his face and ate it. He stroked his cum-covered cock as he straddled me. I suddenly felt him quivering and then heard the first shot of cum hit atop my helmet. The second and third blast covered my stomach and chest as it rolled down my sides. His load was even bigger than Head Gver's or Tayl Tapper's, and that was saying a lot. I had a stupid drunklike smile on my face. Thankfully, the helmet held through the acrobatics.

Phillip collapsed on me, kissing my chest and the nape of my neck. When I opened my eyes, I saw a big dick through the helmet mouth hole pointing at me, accusatorially. It was attached to Azramar. Suddenly, the helmet was pulled off my head. Phillip covered me with his body as if to protect me. He looked into my eyes and seemed to lock on them, I watched mesmerized with my head askew as his pupils dilated and he gave an audible gasp. As I returned his gaze my heart felt as if it leapt out of my chest and a rush came to my brain.

"Dong!" Azramar shouted. "Seize him!"

Chapter 17

Unfortunately for Azramar, he was barefoot and stood on the polished marble bedframe. It was ancient and designed to rock back and forth, which it did the whole time Phillip and I were fucking. I could also see, out of the corner of my eye, that said marble was drenched in Phillip's cum. Apparently, that first blast hit more than my helmet. Phillip rolled off me, which jarred the bed frame where Azramar stood. Azramar flew backwards seemingly swept off his feet. And because a literal orgy had started, no one really listened to him.

"Do you want to live to see tomorrow?" Phillip asked me.

I did not trust him, why should I, yes the sex was hotter than any I had ever experienced in my life and we just had some sort of incredible eye-locking, dopamine-hit-of-a moment once the helmet came off, but hot sex did not equate to, I trust you with my life. This said, what choice did I have? So, I tentatively nodded my head, yes. Without a moment's hesitation, he grasped my hand and pushed through the attendants. Jewels started spilling all over, though one string stayed about his waist. Anyone who pursued might find themselves on the floor on their ass like Azramar, who stepped atop a perfectly rounded gemstone.

"Grab those towels," Phillip said. I dutifully grabbed two towels hanging on hooks and we wiped ourselves off as we ran up a flight of stairs. We passed the lounge, where I stopped long enough to grab the garment bag with my clothes and my phone that I had earlier stashed behind the couch. We then made our way to a service closet and opened the door.

"In here," he commanded.

"Are we just going to hide?" I asked. He shushed me.

"Do you trust me?" he asked.

I didn't, but I responded as honestly as I could. "I don't think I have a choice."

"Good answer," he said. He locked the door from the inside. The closet had a back door that led to a washroom and elegantly appointed office. "My clothes are here. Put them in your bag please," he said as he handed them to me. I did as I was told.

"Shouldn't we dress? I asked.

"No time," he said.

Phillip moved towards the office desk, then came over and put something shiny in the bag. I didn't see what it was, as my adrenaline was rushing at high speed. I just zipped the bag shut and slung it over my shoulder. "Let's go! Back the way we came," he said.

We went back through the restroom and into the closet. Someone was trying to open the door from the other side, but it was locked.

"Get this door open," someone yelled from outside.

"Up the ladder," Phillip said. I hadn't even noticed a ladder when we came through the first time.

"Where does it go?" I asked.

"Up," he said, "Does it matter?"

Up I went. At the top was a circular hatch with a wheel-like valve, similar to what one would find on a bank vault door or a hatch of a submarine. I jerked on it, finally loosened it and then spun it open. The rounded door was heavy. Balancing on a slim ladder in bare feet made me incredibly unstable, but I pushed it open.

As I popped up my head, I was greeted by a much stronger sulfuric smell than I had smelled in the cavern below. The bath, I guessed. I threw the bag up and out onto the floor, climbed out and turned to help Phillip. We quickly shut the hatch behind us and spun it shut and then Phillip jammed a crescent wrench that was lying on the floor through the mechanism of the wheel in attempt to jam it. It definitely looked secure, for now.

"Where are we?" I asked.

"In the bath," he responded.

"I assumed. That's fortunate," I said.

"Yes, but there's a problem," he said.

"What's that?" I asked.

"It's ladies' night and we're not ladies," he replied.

"Follow me," he said.

We skirted along the shadows to a door with printing on it. I didn't read Hungarian, and Hungarian, as stated, is nothing like Russian. "What's it say?" I asked.

"Staff only," he replied. We entered. There were lockers and smocks hanging on the wall and a make-up table.

"Put this on," he said, handing me a smock with urgency.

Hats that resembled shower caps, though they were made of cloth not plastic, hung on hooks. Phillip pointed to one and said, "That too."

"Why?" I asked.

"They're the masseuse's uniforms. I've seen them in photos," he said.

There was a makeup case on the table. He opened it and quickly applied makeup to my face. "Not much," he said. "Just enough to soften the angles," He said as he worked diligently, but also intimately. "The workers will be getting off soon and heading in here shortly," he said. He then applied make-up to his own face.

Just then there was a loud bang followed by a woman's scream. Had our temporary sanctuary been breached? Apparently so, since the next thing we heard was men shouting. This was followed by multiple women yelling in anger. We peeked out and saw pandemonium and chaos ensue. We saw naked men being chased by women clad in smocks similar to the ones we had recently donned. Next, we heard police sirens first in the distance then closer. In all the chaos we decided to make our break.

Chapter 18

Phillip implored, "Grab the bag with our clothes in it," I'm glad he did, as I had nearly forgot it. I grabbed it and we ran. Somehow, dressed in the worst drag possible and with all the chaos, we made it out without getting stopped or questioned.

I called Yuri the minute we turned a corner onto the main drag. He flashed the car's lights once and we made our way toward him. We climbed into the backseat, and we were off into the night.

"Where to?" he asked.

I looked at Phillip unsure. He shouted, "The train station."

"Which one?" Yuri asked. "There are four."

Phillip said, "Nyugati."

"Anything suspicious at the hotel," I queried.

"I don't know," Yuri said. "I went in the back entrance, up the service elevator, and into your room with my master key card, so I didn't see anything. Your suitcase and passport are in the trunk. But the cameras in the hallway surely caught me. I'll probably lie low for the next few days."

Phillip and I busied ourselves changing our clothes in the backseat.

"Here, wipe your face with this," Phillip instructed as he handed me a plastic bottle and a cotton ball.

"What is it?" I asked.

"Makeup remover," he said. "I nicked it from the make-up case back at the bath."

The cotton ball was worthless, so I went to work without it and used one of the discarded smocks as a rag. Eventually we cleaned each other's faces, though in the dark, I'm not sure we did a very good job. "Let's bring this with us, in case we missed some spots" I said, indicating the bottle.

"How do we know there will be a train at this hour and where is a safe place we can even go?" I asked Phillip.

"There is always a train. But I have it on a good authority, that the Central European to Krakow is mysteriously delayed," he replied.

I looked at him confused.

"Undoubtedly because of the *party* we attended tonight," he said with an emphasis on the word party that was not lost on me. "It will conveniently be able to run at 23:05 this evening. We should be able to make it. We'll have to keep a low profile to make sure no one spots us. There will be a few partygoers on it. I'm also sure my HO credit card has been disabled, and if not, better not to use it anyway," he added looking circumspect.

"I can use my Agency card," I said.

"Won't you get in trouble?" he asked a little bit worried.

"As long as you get on the train first, I will be fine." I said.

He looked at me quizzically. "Wherever you go, I have instructions to follow you," I said. I left off the part that my explicit instructions were actually to ride his ass and blow it wide open. Technically, my mission was already accomplished. But, I guessed happily that I still had some more ass-riding to do.

I said thank you and goodbye to Yuri when we arrived at the train station, after he assured me, he would not betray me again. Phillip asked Yuri to look after the Professor, Phillip's boss. The ticket agent in the station spoke German, so given Phillip's fluency, he did the talking. Phillip was now sporting my University of Wisconsin baseball cap, pulled from my suitcase in an attempt to appear incognito. I secretly thanked Johnson for making sure my cover was complete. I sprung for a private sleeping compartment on the train to its final destination, Krakow, but we planned to exit the train in Prague, as Phillip had a trusted friend there. It was only slight subterfuge, but if they spent any time looking for us in Poland, while we were hidden away in the Czech Republic, it was worth the extra cost.

"You will be the only guests in this particular car," the ticket agent said for no apparent reason. Did he want a tip? Deciding I didn't want to risk offending him I slipped him a 10,000 forint note.

We then headed out to the platform, climbed aboard the train, and made our way to our compartment. At exactly 23:05 the train pulled out of the station.

Once our tickets were punched by the porter on duty, we hung the 'Do Not Disturb' sign on the door and our clothes up on hooks in the room. We squeezed our naked selves into the doorframe of our compartment's tiny bathroom, and turned on the shower. The bathroom was so small it doubled as the shower stall. With the removable handheld, adjustable sprayer Phillip directed the water to the corner until it heated up. We buttressed ourselves against the steady rocking of the train, held each other, and said nothing.

While the water warmed, he held me tenderly, as I thought of the harrowing evening we survived. The water took a while. For my part,

I finally felt safe. Once hot, Phillip hung the sprayer on the hook above and the stream of water tumbled over us. We quickly closed the door and proceeded to wash each other, kiss each other, and my cock responded as if on cue. Phillip moved to sit on the edge of the toilet seat and went down on me.

He swallowed the whole length of my shaft to the hilt. Up and down he went on my cock. Was he a sword swallower in his previous life? He slid the tip to his lips, teased the head, which felt incredible, and then plunged the length of it all the way down his throat to my balls. Then he repeated the move over and over again. I don't know how he did it and I didn't necessarily care. He looked up to me all doe-eyed with my cock completely ensnared in his mouth. Then he released it, looked to my eyes, and smiled as the train came to a stop.

"Why are we stopped? I thought this was an express at least to Prague?" I asked.

"Probably the Slovak border," Phillip said. And then, without missing a beat, he returned to sword swallowing. I was so happy that he was a man of many talents and that I was the benefactor of them. I forgot everything–the stopped train, the border, all of it.

I stood him up and kissed him, tasting some of my salty pre-cum in the process. I then turned him around, narrowed the stream of the shower head, and shot it up and around his hole. I then bent him over the toilet, hit my knees, and plunged my tongue deep into his recesses. Then I turned off the shower while I plundered that hole and milked his cock. He moaned with pleasure. Soon he streamed what seemed like gallons of cum, which I collected and rubbed on to my shaft like lube. Then, without missing a beat, I stood up and stuck my cock into his willing hole and fucked him again.

As I did so I wondered, was there an aphrodisiac in the drug they gave me that had incapacitated me earlier. I fucked him and fucked him, in and out. From stern to bow he never once protested as my balls continuously slapped up against his willing ass. It was tight in that little bathroom. My hip bone was against the sink and my butt kept banging against the wall or the door, depending on my angle of entry.

At some point, the train started moving again, as I later recalled I timed my thrusts to the rhythm of the motion. He soon came again, dripping his massive amount of semen into the now open toilet bowl. I didn't have another orgasm that night, but it was not for lack of trying. I think, for the first time in my life my sexual appetite was truly sated.

We turned on the shower again and rinsed off. He then kicked me out of the bathroom, but not before he asked me to borrow my shaving kit, presumably to make use of my toothpaste and other supplies. I didn't care, my tongue, fingers, and cock made use of every part of him. I was as happy as can be. With a grin on my face I started to convert the sofa into a bed. I swaddled myself in one of the luxury robes hanging on the back of the door. A door, on which a light knock now rapped.

I assumed it was the border agent, who probably rode the train across the country, checking papers the whole way, and doing the same on the return trip home. I surveyed the room, all looked normal, as all mayhem up to that moment took place in the tiny bathroom. I grabbed our diplomatic passports, no need to use my no-longer-secret identity, and opened the door. It was not a border agent.

Chapter 19

A syringe attached to a hand flew in and aimed I don't know where. Thankfully my reflexes kicked in and I deflected it. It now was stuck in the wall. My assailant was huge and roughly double my weight. With my other hand fisted, I struck him in the throat. He fell back against the window in the corridor.

My robe fell open and his eyes were drawn to my appendage. With the shift of his gaze, the light from the room caught his face. It was Tayl Tapper and he was pissed, then suddenly distracted. He wore a thin necktie, so I grabbed it, pulled him toward me, rolled back with my feet on his abs, and flipped him over the top of me. He crashed and hit the bathroom door, hard. He was out.

Phillip called out through the closed door, "Everything okay out there?"

"Just making the bed up. I dropped it accidently..."

Getting up off the floor, I looked through the open door and spied Ben Overntakit, who wore brass knuckles and slammed his metal fist into his other open hand. How the fuck did they board this train?

He came toward me and swung. I blocked his swing, ducked in, moved sideways, slipped my arm around his back, shifted my hips and threw him over my shoulder. He was down on top of Tapper, but not out. I grabbed the syringe from the wall and stabbed him with it. I then pushed down on the plunger. That put him out.

"Are you okay!" Phillip yelled.

"Yes!" I called back. "Don't come out yet. I'm afraid I've made a mess of things."

Tapper was moaning. I reached in his jacket pocket. As I suspected – a second syringe. I administered it to him. I then emptied their pockets, of their phones, wallets, passports, and put it all in my bag. That should slow them down when they come to. I had no idea what was in the syringe, so I didn't know when they'd come to. I bound their wrists and feet with anything at my disposal like Tayl's tie, the robe from my bathrobe, etc. Their socks made for good gags. I quietly lowered the top bunk and heaved them both up there. That wasn't easy. I then shoved it closed. It took a few pushes. I hope I didn't break anything, on the train that is. I quickly straightened up the room and tied my robe shut with the rope from the other robe hanging on the back of the door.

I knew the room next door was empty. I went over there; the lower bunk was already made up, literally with two mints on the pillow. So, I moved our stuff over there and then returned to our compartment. I acted like I didn't have a care in the world and I waited for Phillip. Finally, he exited the bathroom. Looking like a tired ray of sunshine. I realized, in that moment that I too was exhausted.

"I thought you were making up the bed." He paused, confused. Then asked, "Where are our clothes?"

"I was," I said. "But when I dropped the upper bunk down... Well let's just say there's a couple of foul things up there. I think it's best that we move next door. I already made the lower bed up. We can cuddle there, if you're up for it."

"If you think it's okay to move, I'm okay with that. I'm definitely up for cuddling." he said. He grabbed the ticket on the door as we exited, presumably to move it to the room next door.

"I'd leave it. If you don't mind," I said. "It might be safer, if we're in a room no one knows were in," I added.

"Who's going to find us here? He asked perplexed as he replaced the ticket.

"Probably, no one. But just in case," I said. It was then I came to realize Phillip's *friends* were much more dangerous than I ever anticipated.

We moved to the new compartment. I hung the robe and he hung the towel in which he had been wrapped. We then collapsed on the lower bunk, entwined in each other's arms, naked. Through pillow talk, we recounted the evenings events and laughed at how I came to steal the show, with his help of course, earlier that evening. Slowly, I nodded off and fell into a deep slumber.

When I awoke, I panicked. Phillip wasn't there. My fears were allayed when he popped in the door with a plastic tray laden with coffee and an assortment of European breakfast foods. "You're awake," he said with a big smile. "Breakfast is served. The dining car was about to close and I figured you were likely famished. So, I thought I'd better grab some." He was so adorable. We'll be in Prague in less than an hour.

I was starving. Other than the protein shake, fruit, and cheese last night, I didn't eat anything since yesterday morning. I grabbed some cold cuts and wrapped them in cheese and popped them in my mouth. "We need to make a plan," he said.

"Hold that thought," I said, as I slurped down some coffee. "I have to pee." I slipped into this compartment's immaculate bathroom and drained my hog.

Over breakfast, we had a bit of an argument. I wanted to go to Interpol and take Azramar down. "They tried to rape me," I exclaimed.

"Did they rape you?" Phillip asked.

"No, but only because I outsmarted them. But, they did rape Yuri," I said.

"Who is this Yuri, again? Phillip asked.

"He's the guy who took us to the train station last night. The guy from the hotel you bribed," I said.

"Didn't he betray you?" Phillip asked, feigning innocence.

"Well, yea. But rape? I think that's a little harsh," I responded.

"I think he got what he deserved. But that's me," Phillip said.

"No one deserves rape, Phillip," I said sharply.

Phillip quieted and then removed the now empty tray from my lap, the remnants of breakfast contained upon it. He knelt before me, rubbing my thighs and getting me hard in the process. He definitely had figured out quickly how to soften my edges. Then he asked, "What do you think about taking them down from the inside, or making them legit?" This he said with a bit of a wicked smile.

"What do you mean?" I asked.

He continued, "I knew I was being investigated shortly after you learned you were to investigate me. When you were probing my drive, I was notified. I also had your number a long time before you had mine."

"I don't believe it," I said.

"Believe me or don't believe me. But when Azramar said HO infiltrated every level of government and every organization, which includes the Agency; he was not lying. I saw you on that plane from Washington, I knew who you were, and why you were there."

"You're kidding me." I said, shocked.

"Unfortunately, I am not," he said. "You contact Interpol when we arrive in Prague, and they will thank you and assure you this will be investigated. They will ask you if you are safe and will offer to come and get you. Next, you will be driven, not to Interpol's local office, but to HO headquarters in Prague and eventually into Azramar's hands." He kissed me on my stomach and hugged me. I was confused but comforted at the same time.

"Are they fucking everywhere?" I asked.

"They are in every city of merit around the world. In this case, merit is a loose term. They are everywhere they need to be from fashionable capitals to sleepy forgotten towns at the end of a dirt road in the hinterlands," he said. "As we like to say, the sun never sets on the HO globe."

"So, what do we do?" I asked despondently.

"As I said, I have a friend in Prague. He'll know what to do." In the meantime, we're going to lie low and off the grid."

"I'm not good at camping," I said.

He laughed. "I meant it metaphorically, not literally. I know a hostel, really more of a dorm where we can stay. It'll be best to avoid hotels," he added.

When the train pulled into the station, we restored the room as best we could and left another 10,000 Forint note, as a tip. When we exited the train, the porter approached us. "Gentlemen," he queried, "I thought you were traveling through to Krakow."

"We are," I lied. "But we're going to check some of our luggage here at the station as we'll be coming back this way in a few weeks. Can you do us a favor, by the way?"

"Yes of course," he said.

"We're still exhausted," I said. "Can you just let us sleep through to Krakow."

"I get off the train here," he said. "But I can absolutely let my replacement know."

"That would be great," I replied with a kind, sincere smile. "Thank you."

We exchanged the remainder of our Hungarian forints and U.S. dollars for Czech koruny, the local currency, since we were going to need to be operating on a cash-only basis for the foreseeable future. We then grabbed a taxi out in front of the station and Phillip gave the driver directions to the Větrník neighborhood. We proceeded west from the train station and up a hill. After a streetcar passed, I looked back through the rear window. The scene looked straight out of a fairytale. No wonder they call it the city of one-hundred spires.

When we arrived at the hostel/dorm, Phillip got us a room under a fake name telling the guy at the desk that we were German students. The attendant was far more interested in his television program than he was in us, which was a good thing. It was 10:30 a.m. We got to the room, which was up one flight of stairs and unlocked the door with one of the two keys we had been given.

It was spartan. It actually very much resembled an American-style dorm room with two single beds on either side, two desks adjacent to the head of the beds and two closets a foot or two away from the base of the beds, and a window on the far wall. It was a sunny and breezy fall day. Light danced around the room from the trees which were undulated by the wind. I locked the door behind us. Though it may have been a false sense, I finally felt safe. Though I felt that way before, only to have reality, or in this case a needle shoved in my face, this was different somehow.

We dragged one of the beds to the other side of the room, making the two single beds into a double. We laid down and both reached for the other at the same time and stared at the ceiling.

"So now what?" I said. "Do we call your friend?"

"Perhaps, perhaps not. I don't know..." Phillip said with a coy smile. "I do have my best ideas when I'm being fucked..."

That's all I needed to hear. I quickly started unbuttoning his shirt and unzipping his pants, while I raced to take my own clothes off. I did take one moment to close the curtains. That taken care of, we proceeded to fuck and fuck.

We fucked with pure unadulterated abandon, best of all with no stupid helmet and no tiny bathroom to constrain us. I fucked his face first. Well, he was on his knees on the bed, and I stood on it with him in front of me. I then tongue-fucked his hole again. I loved that hole. Then I slam-fucked him up against the dorm room wall. I fucked him with his head and neck on a pillow on the floor, ass in the air, me with my feet on either side of his hips, doing something akin to squats, with my dick plunging in and out of his ass. I eventually pulled out shooting cum all over him.

He was so hot and horny. I had already come twice in the last 18 or so hours. He begged, "Eat my ass, please. I of course, heartily obliged.

On to my second favorite thing to do in bed. I lay flat on my back on the bed and he rode my face.

I just watched as his cheeks enveloped both halves of my face and looked up his sexy muscled back massaging it. He played with my cock, which I could tell was still leaking cum. He started sucking on it and began to shoot streams of cum all over my chest while he bounced at high velocity on my stiff tongue. Once more it seemed like gallons of cum spilled out over me and dripped down my sides. Afterward, more cum and still more cum. When we were finished, I expected him to want to cuddle, but instead he shouted, "I have a plan!"

Chapter 20

He may have a plan, but we were covered in cum and needed to hit the shower. Fortunately, there was no one in the hallway. Wrapped only in towels, we made our way down to the shower room with no issues. While I tried to keep the cum from getting on the towel cinched around my waist, I had to keep scooping the cum up with my fingers before it reached the towel or dripped on to the floor. I slurped every drop. Damn, he tasted good.

Thankfully, the shower room was empty when we arrived. We were washing ourselves but found it hard to keep our hands off each other. For efficiency's sake, at least that's what I told myself, I decided to soap him up which allowed me to have my hands all over his taut body and rounded ass. He returned the favor but tended to mostly play with my cock. I think he found it fascinating, but certainly not overwhelming, which just made me happy.

At one point we heard a woman's voice, "Mushu?" she called.

"Ne," Phillip responded in the deepest voice I'd ever heard him emit.

That was that. "What did she want?" I asked.

"To join us, but she would only if we were women," he said matter-of-factly.

We returned to the room, dried ourselves off, got dressed. He outlined a plan and checked in with me all along the way. It wasn't foolproof, but thankfully, as Phillip explained, "it only has to be Azramar-proof."

"Look, Azamar is a bit of a pawn," he explained. "Each continent has a director, and Azramar is in charge of the European continent and the UK. There's been a power struggle for the top."

"The top?" I asked quizzically.

"Well, unfortunately, the patriarchy is alive and well, even in HO," Phillip said.

"No surprise, it's all men," I said.

"If it were only that simple, and thus everyone would be treated equally. But it's a little more insidious than that," Phillip said. "Only power tops can have leadership positions. Because of that Azramar is limited to this area. As a bottom, I am free to traverse the globe so I know all the HO movers and shakers across it. I've never met the Magnus Gallus, he's sort of the Top Cock, if you will. I've seen him a few times, but he's always masked or in the shadows. Mask or no mask, he's ancient."

"This is fascinating, but sort of scary at the same time," I said. "The fact that this has gone on for literally thousands of years and the world is none the wiser is frightful."

"Well now you know," he said. "I say you take this knowledge and sign up. Become a figurative card-carrying member of HO. As a power top with an absolutely stunning appendage..." He stopped for a moment and just stared at my package, "...who is a stallion in bed. You, with my help of course, could rise to be the Top Cock one day and I could be your consort, if you'll have me. We would be the number one secret gay couple in the world."

I can't say I wasn't intrigued. After all, Phillip may not yet be the love of my life, but the fact that he could take me and seemed genuinely interested in doing so... Well, I was falling pretty, hard.

"Once there," he continued, "you could initiate reform and make HO better."

"But you don't even know me," I said. "Don't get me wrong, sex with you is so amazing. I mean I will follow you to the ends of the Earth, but—"

"—Mr. Don Kee Dong, I know everything about you. I have been studying you since you walked into the doors of the Agency four years ago. I tripled my studies once I came under your scrutiny. I've spied you in the gym at the cafeteria, though somehow that appendage escaped me." This he said while licking his lips and once again staring at my crotch.

"No way," I said. "I would notice you. "There is no way that ass would ever escape my detection."

"Well, discretion is my job," he said. "I am HO's eyes and ears at the Agency's DC office. If HO needs me somewhere, the orders, allegedly from the Agency, come down and I go. I've never spotted anyone else at the Agency with a HO mark, but I'm convinced I'm not the only one. Look, it's a two-thousand-year-old organization. You don't have that kind of staying power unless you put smart people in important roles and observe absolutely everything."

I countered this with, "But HO more closely resembles a criminal enterprise than not. I have trouble with that." I said, almost pleading, I guess for permission, though I'm not sure I knew that at the time.

"I won't say they're all good, but during various purges such as the Inquisition and the Holocaust, HO saved countless lives." Phillip implored. "Gay people may have been revered, or at least tolerated during the Greek and Roman Empires, but that was about the last time. HO got thousands of queers and Jews out of Nazi Germany alone, and not only their members. There's still a world of good that can come from HO. Gay hating authoritarian governments are still popping up all over the globe. So there is plenty of noble work yet to do. You are not going to be able to bring HO down from the outside. You could however reform it, or if you feel it is unsalvageable, bring it down from the inside. I just ask that you take a chance on HO and on me."

He had these puppy dog eyes that just made me want to cradle him, and possibly do other things, but that could wait for now.

"I am pledged only to HO members," he said.

"What?" I asked. "But you had sex with me, three times or so, and forgive me for noticing but you sure seemed like you were enjoying it," I said.

"Well, I didn't know it was you and you bore the HO mark though, after two showers, it appears to fade..." He said this while picking up my left hand and looking at the faded penmanship from yesterday, "...and you have been anointed as a HO member, which is the first step to being admitted to HO."

"Anointed? Come again?" I asked incredulously. "No one has anointed me."

"Yes, you were, by your masseur Sergey, the other night at the bath," he responded. "Did not your masseur shoot semen on you while reciting 'Unxi Te'? He reported that he did so."

"I mean, yeah. He came on my head, which I thought was weird, though kind of hot at the same time. He mumbled something, but I couldn't make it out."

"What he mumbled," Phillip said a little annoyed, "was, I anoint you, in Latin, 'Unxi Te.' It was your masseur's semen that anointed you. He singled you out for HO, I mean with that cock of yours he did exactly what he was instructed to do when he was indoctrinated into the organization, though he had no idea HO already had their eyes on you... that I already had my eyes on you."

"I'll have to think about all this. It's a lot." I said.

"That's understandable, but don't think too long." Phillip said. "I guarantee HO, and its informants, are currently conducting a dragnet across Eastern Europe, looking for us.

"You think he wants to kill us?" I asked.

"After that performance last night, and me..." he now mocked Azramar in a not very good Spanish accent, saying "HO's most prize ass, er asset." Then he became serious. "No, he doesn't want to kill us. If you were to go to Interpol, and try to destroy 2,000+ years of HO, there is no place on this planet you could go where you would be safe."

"You watch too many spy movies, my friend," I said with a chuckle.

"I wish that were the case," Phillips said. "I'm afraid it is not an exaggeration."

"We have no bargaining power. How can we move forward?" I stammered.

"There you're wrong," Phillip said. "Azramar is, what Americans would call, 'a nice piece of real estate, but with no improvements.' Our main task is to make sure Azramar does not lose face. He is a fragile man with a fragile ego. If we make him look like the hero of the story, we can move forward and get what we want."

When I expressed confusion, he elaborated. "He's not the sharpest tool in the HO shed. HO would love nothing more than to bring you into their fold. But Azramar is not going to trust you at first. He knows you are investigating HO.

"That's not true," I protested. "I am investigating you. I merely stumbled across HO in the process."

"I am taken care of regardless. HO will see to that. You can turn me in if you like. It's a small price to pay to protect the legacy of HO."

"That seems harsh," I said. "As far as I can see, you haven't been pocketing money. You've just took advantage of enviable discounts."

"What can I say? I have expensive tastes, and HO wants me in the position working with the Undersecretary because they believe in his work. They want him to be comfortable and healthy. The Undersecretary is brilliant, but he is a bit of an absent-minded professor. He doesn't pay attention to either what I do or where I go. But he's also kind of helpless. Before breakfast, I had to call him from the train and arrange his day for him. He's familiar with the hotel and the UN Centre, so he'll be fine.

In a panic, I asked. "Your phone, it could be tracking us right now. Where is it?"

"Right where it should be. Halfway to Krakow. I left it on the train," he said with a smile. "As I was saying, the professor enjoys the finer things in life. He thinks I walk on water."

"You do," I quipped, but then added, "I'm not convinced I'm enough bargaining power. So, other than your hot ass on my fat cock, what's our secret weapon?"

"That office we were in last night..."

"After I made incredible love to you?" I asked.

"Yes, that office. It's Azramar's Budapest office," Phillip said smiling. "While you were grabbing your clothes, I grabbed Azramar's hard drive."

"How? You didn't have time to open his computer up and disconnect his internal hard drive." I asked and stated.

"Remember when I said he's not too bright?" he asked.

"A few times." I said.

"Well, he keeps all his HO data on an unencrypted external hard drive, which he normally keeps on his person. But when he's naked, like last night, that's a little hard to do. So, I spotted it plugged into his computer last night and I grabbed it." Phillip then held it up. "And here it is. It should hold some, if not all, the keys to HO. I also have these," he said, holding up a length of gleaming diamonds. The ones that circled his waist last night as I had fucked him while in the cavern. "He's definitely going to want these back, as they were only on loan."

He stood up and walked to where our jackets hung on hooks near the door and said, "We're going to put on our coats and head to an internet cafe. We will upload a copy of the hard drive to an Agency server that only I have access to, so we have a copy. We will meet with Azramar in a very public place and detail our terms of surrender for you to join HO or, if you prefer, I can meet with him alone and you can go back to DC and report me. However you wish to proceed. If you choose to join HO, we will force Azramar to solidify the terms with the Magnus Galus' people. Then, and only then will we return the drive and the gems to him."

I ignored Phillip's comment about turning him in and just asked, "Won't he assume we made a copy of the hard drive? He must know it's gone."

"I'm sure he realizes it's missing, whether he knows one can make a copy, that remains to be determined." Phillip said. "The important thing is we allow him to save face. He's the hero of the story. If there's a hint of a double cross, we let him know we'll release the contents of the drive onto the Dark Web. Shall we go?" he asked.

"You're amazing," I said.

"How so?" he asked.

"You came up with all that while a giant cock was plowing your ass," I said.

He replied with a smile, "I told you, I have my best ideas while I'm getting fucked!"

Chapter 21

At the internet café, Phillip viewed the contents of the hard drive and said to me, "This is better than I could've dreamed. Everything is here. If HO headquarters knew how cavalier he was with their data, they'd have his cockhead."

Phillip used a TOR browser to upload the files to a server only he had access to at the Agency back in DC. He sent three emails using his HO email account. The first was to HO headquarters in New York City requesting a video meeting at 10 a.m. EST tomorrow; the second to his friend in Prague who he said he trusted implicitly and who could host the meeting; the third to Azramar. In that final email, Phillip said he had convinced me to negotiate my surrender to HO and that Azramar's hard drive and some of the diamonds were in Phillip's possession in order to ensure our mutual safety.

He wrote that the hard drive and gemstones would be returned to him intact once we negotiated terms at a rendezvous point tomorrow at 13:00 Prague time. We were, per Phillip, to meet him at Prague Castle, the city's most famous landmark and Azramar was to come alone.

We headed back to the dorm for a nap and some afternoon delight. Later, we went to a family-owned restaurant for a dinner of guláš, a

Czech stew with tender beef, paprika, onion, and bread dumplings, which was absolutely delicious. We made it an early night with more sleep, naked, and once again wrapped in each other's arms. I didn't dare turn on my cellphone or the two I had pocketed on the train lest they were tracked.

We arrived the next day at Prague Castle via Tram 2 at 12:45. The rendezvous point was the Singing Fountain in the Royal Gardens adjacent to the castle.

Phillip kissed me and said, "I suspect, even though I told him to come alone, Azramar will have some colleagues lurking about. I'm aware of your skills. Would you take care of them, please, and then join us by that fountain," he said pointing to a fountain in the distance.

"Sure," I said, as he handed me a dozen zip ties. "Where did those come from?" I asked as I pondered how a man who thinks of everything is a man who lives in my heart.

"I was in the Dutch version of the boy scouts as a youth and our motto was, '*Weest Paraat*," he said.

What does it mean? I queried.

"Be prepared," he said resolutely.

"When you return from surveilling the perimeter and neutralizing any threats, go to those shrubs by the fountain," he said as he pointed towards some bushes. He continued, "Give me one of your bird whistles if you want to turn me into the Agency, go on with your life without me, and without HO. Or two whistles if you want to join forces and take HO on from the inside."

I was stunned by his statement, but all I could think to say was, "How do you know I do bird whistles? Never mind," I quickly added.

I loved his confidence in me. Before I could say anything more, he was off moving toward the fountain.

In very ninja fashion I walked the perimeter of the grounds. I found three men in three different locations with the telltale signs: HO tattoos. The first two had tattoos on their left hands. The third on his right. I quickly took out the first two. Slipped up, placed in chokehold, and they were out. I zip-tied the first guy to a park bench and the second to a fence. Too easy.

I then tried the same move on the third guy with no such luck. He quickly slipped out of my hold, adopted a karate stance and attacked. I blocked him blow for blow and narrowly missed getting punched in the face. His problems were twofold: Kung Fu and Jiu-Jitsu are far more dangerous than karate and Comrade Wakacokski had taught my classmates and me to fight very, very dirty. If he said it once, he said it one hundred times, "when someone is trying to kill you, there is no such thing as honor."

The third HO man tried to distract me by running up my back and wrapping his thighs around my neck. He started to squeeze. We both fell to the ground. I punched him in his ribs and broke free. We both stood up, but I held a handful of dirt while he glared at me, rubbing his throat. I went in as if to punch with my left and instead I threw the dirt in his eyes with my right. I then broke his kneecap. That'll hurt, I thought. As if on cue, he screamed in pain. I punched him in the windpipe. I felt bad, but with all the tourists around, I needed to silence the scream. The blow had the desired effect. He went down. He was wearing a tie, so I gagged him with it. He literally tried to bite me. I zip-tied him to a park bench with his back to the castle and out of frustration, delivered a roundhouse kick to his head which knocked him unconscious. I cleaned myself off as best as I could and headed for the rendezvous point. I felt bad, but biting someone? That's beyond dirty, not to mention, unsanitary.

I stopped short of the fountain's clearing and stood behind the large shrub and gave one bird whistle alerting Phillip to my presence. This was followed by a long pause that contained the weight of my destiny, and then a second bird whistle. I could just hear their conversation over the joint babble of the tourists and the fountain.

"I convinced Dong that HO is the side that always wins." Phillip said. "You are right about him, but he wasn't ordered to investigate HO, he was ordered to investigate me. He didn't even know HO existed until you told him. I believe he is willing to exonerate me, but if not, I will pay the price, not HO.

"How can I trust you or him?" Azramar said. "I can't believe you aided and abetted him last night. You stole my hard drive and half the diamonds. And you! I had to fly here from Krakow this morning."

"Why were you in Krakow?" Phillip asked, feigning confusion.

"You know very well, why I was in Krakow," he said rolling his eyes. "Poor Ben and Tayl. They are both going to need hours of therapy for PTSD."

"Manuel, your bravado often gets the better of you. I was afraid you might kill him in the heat of the moment," Phillip said. "That's also why I took your hard drive, and the diamonds were tied around my waist, at your urging, I might add. They merely came with as we exited the cavern. When this is all over, and Dong and I are safe, I will return all of it to you."

"¡Dios Mio! You are the worst!" Manuel said.

"Am I, really? Because from where I'm standing, and as far as our members are aware, did they even know anything was amiss last night? I mean, they got one a hell of a show." This brought a smile to my face and caused my cock to stir.

"It was muy bueno," Azramar proclaimed. "I mean, did you get a load of that cock?"

"A couple of times," Phillip said matter-of-factly. "Do you want to throw that away? Imagine the credit you'll get, your team discovering the owner of the true Kong Dong in all its massive glory." This Phillip said with the bravado of an admiral describing the launch of a new class of destroyers. "And he wants to join us."

"I don't know," Azramar said. "He embarrassed me."

"To you, Manuel. Not to anyone else." Phillip said kindly with a tinge of sadness in his voice. "Will you think about it Manuel and let me know? We're in Prague for another day. We can get on a call with the MG's team and work out the details."

"Un momento," Azramar said as he pulled out his cellphone from his jacket pocket and hit a button just as I walked forward out of the bushes. I held up three fingers to Phillip, indicating three assailants and then dragged my finger across my neck. Phillip blanched. He must've thought I'd killed them. I quickly shook my head no, and then I mimed that they were merely, 'asleep.' Azramar was too busy with his phone to notice any of this.

"Team-leader, why are you not responding?" Azramar shouted at the phone.

"Manuel, I asked you to come alone, but you ignored that request," Phillip said calmly. "The people you are trying to reach have been neutralized."

"¿Qué pasa?" he asked. "Who did this?"

"Dong," Phillip said. "A man of many talents who could be very useful to HO."

"Dong!" Azramar spit out. "Never!" as he glared contemptuously at me.

Phillip, who had been sitting on the fountain's edge, stood to leave.

"I won't be seeing you again, Señor Azramar, as I cannot trust you." Phillip said coldly. "Either we can get together with the MG's office via secure video link or not. I've scheduled a call at 1600 Prague time today. We can talk then, as you are welcome to join, or not at all. If you choose to join, here is the link," Phillip said as he handed him a piece of paper.

"Wait, wait..." Azramar cried out.

"Sorry, we have somewhere to be." Phillip said. "Think about what's best for you and for HO. You can explain how you lost their most treasured asset and their secrets, or how you kept it all in the fold and found the asset's most perfect counterpart. Adios amigo."

As we parted together, hand in hand, I looked over my shoulder at Azramar. He stared incredulously at us. Or, was he perhaps staring incredulously at Phillip's survivalist ass? Either way, he was incredulous.

Chapter 22

After Prague Castle, Phillip thought it was best to check in on his boss. As previously reported, he usually had to somewhat babysit him and Phillip hadn't seen him in nearly 48 hours. Per the conference schedule, they should currently be on a break. With our current location, just outside Prague Castle, not a secret since we just left Azramar, I turned on my phone and handed it to Phillip.

He punched in the professor's mobile number. I previously called in a favor to Yuri from the dorm's front desk to ask him to keep an eye on the professor, as well. I asked him to take him to his meetings and dinner engagements. I was still pissed at him, but that didn't mean he didn't still owe me.

The phone rang and the professor answered. "Herr Professor," Phillip said, "Are you at the conference center with no problems?" I listened in with my cheek brushing up against Phillip and his beautifully soft hair.

"Ja, ja, dear boy, you spoil me. I never have to think of anything but my work," the Undersecretary said.

"You are set for dinner with the missions from South Africa and Brazil this evening?" Phillip inquired. "Now I know you like your beef but do consider fish this evening. You know it agrees with you more.

I picked this restaurant out, especially for you, as they are known for flying in their seafood fresh every day. The maître d' is a good friend, so he will take good care of you. The car will pick you up in front of the conference centre. Take a couple of the South Africans or the Brazilians in the car with you." Phillip said the latter, so as to keep the professor safe with companions, I assumed.

"Good idea, my dear boy. We'll save the planet one taxi ride at a time." The professor said. "Now I know you spent summers here whilst in school. Go spend time with your friends. I'll be fine. Do not worry about me, besides I am here with one of your friends now."

Phillip grew worried. "Which friend might that be professor?"

"A nice young man, Ilov from Bulgaria," the professor said.

"Oh my," Phillip said with a look of panic, but composure in his voice.

"I haven't talked to him the whole conference professor, can you put him on, please?" Phillip asked.

The Bulgarian Ilov Giandik came on the phone, "Azramar is looking for you," Ilov said coldly with a little bitchiness thrown in.

"Funny," Phillip replied, "I just left him at the Castle. I guess he found me."

"You're in, how do the Americans say, deep-shit, Mihol!," said Ilov.

"Don't worry, Ilov. I'm very good with a shovel. Also, Ilov," Phillip continued, "My boyfriend here has taken out five HO operatives in the past day or so. That makes the score Giandik: one, Dong five. I'd watch your back going forward if I were you. He's still a little sore at you, since you were the last one he spoke with before waking up naked and strapped to a chair."

Ilov said no more. The professor came back on the phone. "What did you say to him?" I heard the professor say with a chuckle in his voice. "He turned three shades of white and scurried away."

"I told him he is not my friend and to stay away from you." Phillip said. "You are far too important for the likes of him."

"You worry too much my boy. But as you say, I will avoid him," The professor said.

Phillip was worried for the professor's safety, especially given the unpredictability of Azramar. Being an Undersecretary of a UN agency offered the illusion of safety, but no more than that. "Thank you. Enjoy dinner sir and stay safe."

"Thank you, Phillip." The professor said. "Have a good afternoon and evening and don't you worry about me."

"I'm headed north to see some friends sir, so I will not be joining you on the flight home, but everything was arranged. Are you good to get home on your own sir?" Phillip asked.

"My boy, believe it or not I survived for decades before you became my assistant and besides you made all the arrangements. I will make it. Don't you worry."

"Very well. Thank you, sir. Please take care.
Auf wiedersehen." Phillip hung up. He was a little misty-eyed.

To help change his mood, I changed the subject. "Ah, you called me your boyfriend to Ilov," I said as I smiled unabashedly. "You did it for effect, didn't you?"

"I did. And I'm aware I've sprung a lot on you lately, but take some time to think about it. By the way, I would be honored to be your boyfriend," Phillip said.

Chapter 23

We turned off the phone, then departed the Castle grounds, and headed via the tram for the Czech National Library, where Phillip's friend worked, to make use of their video-conferencing facilities.

We arrived early so we gave ourselves a self-guided tour of the courtyard and buildings, some modern, some very old world. The oldest section had ornate bookcases with massive hand-carved wood pillars, a row of old globes and clocks down a center aisle that went on for miles, and a beautifully hand-painted ceiling, as if Michaelangelo had one day stopped by on his way back to Rome. When it was close to the time for our call, Phillip approached the Head Librarian's office.

"Mr. Mihol, so nice to see you again." The handsome secretary at the office counter said. "Is Head Cumspiller expecting you?" the young secretary, queried.

"Yes." Phillip said. "I wrote him yesterday. I'm hopeful he might be free to meet with us." Just then a very trim and well-dressed man, probably in his mid-40s entered the office.

"Phillip, so good to see you," he said with much enthusiasm as he kissed each of Phillip's cheeks. It was then that I spied the HO tattoo on his left hand and the huge penis lines visible through his tight slacks. Phillip returned the kisses, as I pondered: had Phillip been with him before? I dismissed the question immediately. "Please, please come into my office." He ushered us in and shut the door behind us, then turned to me and said, "Hi, I'm Wåktor Cumspiller, the Head Librarian here. You are?"

"Oh, sorry," Phillip stammered. "I was just so relieved to see you. This is my..." Phillip paused, "My friend Don Kee Dong. He was initiated into HO the other evening." While Phillip said this, I worried. *Could this guy be trusted?*

"Oh, this is The Kong Dong," he squealed with delight. "I heard you two put on quite the show the other night. You are the talk of Eastern Europe, actually, all of Europe at this point. I'm just sorry I couldn't be there. My daughter had a recital," he said, as he ushered us to a comfortable sitting area.

I blushed as Phillip put his right hand on my knee. I focused on the O of the HO of Phillip's tattoo and thought of his tight hole and had to shift a bit uncomfortably in my chair as my cock started to react to my musings.

"I was surprised, when you said you would be, how did you say, 'in the neighborhood.' You're not running off to join the circus or anything, are you?" he asked a bit uncomfortably.

"Oh no," Phillip said. "We're quite happy with the HO circus we're in. But as I said in my email yesterday, I do need a secure connection to the New York office to negotiate Dong's package. He is a once in a lifetime find. Azramar really deserves all the credit. I'm just here to look out for Dong's interest. As you've told us time and time again, library lines are the most secure."

"Anonymous and secure, and all record of the call once completed are wiped from the memory after each use," Cumspiller said. "I'm so glad you came to me, so few do. I've told them, as you said, come to the library when you need to call home. Do you have an appointed time?"

"It's in 20 minutes. Please forgive us for such short notice," Phillip said apologetically.

"Not to worry," Cumspiller said. "Librarians are here to serve, and I would do anything in my power for our most treasured asset." He looked at Phillip practically licking his lips. They definitely have fucked, I thought. Just like that, the jealousy was back.

The Head Librarian picked up his desk phone, punched a few buttons and started barking orders in English into the phone.

I whispered to Phillip, "He doesn't speak Czech?"

"He's a Dane," whispered Phillip in reply.

"Come. We don't have much time," the librarian said. As we departed his office he told his assistant he'd be back shortly and we exited the office suite. We took a set of stairs down one floor and made our way to a conference room. We were definitely in the newer part of the building now.

Once we arrived to a conference room, technicians were setting up some equipment. Cumspiller asked of the technicians, "Are we good to go? These gentlemen are from the U.N."

After the technicians left, Cumspiller said, "Just trying to keep up appearances." He gave Phillip a hug and two pecks, one on each cheek, and a too-long hug, in my opinion. Surprisingly, he hugged me and kissed me on both cheeks as well.

"You should return to Prague soon," he said. "We could have a very good time. There is a dungeon in the basement of the old library building." He was looking at Phillip when he said this. He quickly added, "The three of us, that is." This he said while looking at me up and down while manhandling his stiffening cock with one hand and adjusting his tortoise shells with the other.

"Well, I leave you men to it. Good luck," Cumspiller the lustful librarian said as he exited.

Chapter 24

Once he was gone, Phillip turned to me and asked, "Do you trust me?"

Yes," I replied. Without a word, he kissed me.

The video conference started promptly at 1600 hours Central European Standard Time. On the call, at least per the names on the screen were I.R.A. Cumdumpster, Rim Mycheex, and Duncan Thispol, and of course, the one and only Manuel Azramar. There was also a blank box with no name listed, so I ignored it.

Duncan was clearly in charge. "Azramar, congratulations," Duncan said. "All we've heard out of Budapest is how your Autumnal Equinox celebration was the best ever. It's the talk around the HO-Globe.

"Thank you," Azramar replied. "I appreciate that."

"I see Phillip, our number one asset in all his glory on the call as well," Duncan said as Phillip pulled me into the frame of the screen. "And is this the now HO-Globe famous, Kong Dong of Europe? Based on what I've heard of his performance, he may be able to go for the HO-Globe title next year, not just the European one. It's an honor to meet you, albeit virtually," Duncan said excitedly.

"The pleasure is all mine, gentlemen," I said. "Please call me Don Kee Dong.

Mr. Cumdumpster suddenly piped up, "Such stamina we hear."

"Yes, we cannot wait to meet you in person, Mr. Dong," said Mycheex. "After your performance in Budapest, and the scuttlebutt I'm hearing, half of HO wants a piece of Dong and the other half a piece of Mihol." Cumdumpster said, with a little too much enthusiasm, as he put a finger to his lips and seemed to nibble at the tip.

"Phillip, thank you for bringing out the best in Mr. Dong." Duncan said.

"Just doing my HO part," Phillip said and quickly added, "but the credit all goes to Azramar. He orchestrated the whole thing, and he's the one that worked so hard to get Don Kee Dong on board. He practically had him over a barrel."

"Azramar, is that true?" Duncan asked.

Azramar responded, "I don't know that I'd say all that."

"Of course it's true. You Spanish men, so modest," Phillip lied. "The credit clearly goes to Azramar," Phillip then scratched on a piece of paper and slid it so it was right in front of me. It read, 'are you ok to join HO?' I nodded my head in the affirmative.

"Duncan, you know, I enjoy serving under you and have always admired your leadership." Phillip said. He buttered people up so well, I had learned. He added, "I think Dong deserves a special place in HO.

"Of course, Phillip," Duncan said. "I think I speak for all of us when I say, we want Dong in HO."

"Oh, yes," Phillip continued. "I think everyone's on board with that, including Don Kee Dong. When I say special place, I mean as part of the protectorate with full access, the right to test initiates, conduct recruitment, and have guest star roles at ceremonies across the HO Globe.

"I don't know Phillip, that's a long list," Duncan said.

Phillip countered, "Dong has the tool to match that long list. Further, based on my primary research, in addition to his girth, length, and stamina, all of which I have personally tested. Trust me when I say, there is no one I've come across at HO that has outmatched him." Both Duncan and Azramar blanched at this comment, while Cumdumpster and Mycheeks looked like they had switched their vibrators from low to high, as they both lit up like disco balls.

"I'm not done with my list Duncan," Phillip continued. "First, qualifications: this based on my secondary research. Dong possesses a Master's in Finance from MIT, his CPA credential, a Bachelor's in International Relations from Dartmouth. He is also fluent in English, Russian, French, and Vietnamese. He is a master of jiu-jitsu and kung fu..."

Ah, now he laid it on thick, I wouldn't say master... blackbelt would be the better descriptor.

"...and he is an expert practitioner of a Russian fighting style called SAMBO. Did I mention his Dong of Death? Need I show you what's left of my rapturous hole?"

Cumdumpster and Mycheeks let out involuntary high-pitched squeals at that last part.

"No, thank you, Phillip, that won't be necessary," Duncan said, his voice quivering slightly.

"Then, please allow me to cover his suggested package," Phillip said. Cumdumpster looked a bit aghast at this. But Phillip continued undaunted. "We should compensate him $30,000 USD annually for incidentals. This, of course, in addition to his Agency salary, his residence should be moved into the HO building where I live in Dupont

Circle in DC. The apartment next to me is currently vacant. He needs a promotion at the Agency because he is underutilized there, and he would be of less use to us if left in his current position."

Phillip continued undaunted, "He is better suited to the agency's field investigation unit. This will make him more mobile to HO, get him closer to the top of the Agency, and offer greater access to information that could be of use to us. I'm aware this will take some time,"

Phillip paused for a breath and took a swig of water. "I also believe a personal orientation by Cumdumpster and Mycheex would be the best way to bring Dong up to speed." Cumdumpster and Mycheex perked up at this suggestion and looked giddy with anticipation.

"Look, you all said the reports have been rolling in. I believe he could be the one many of us have been looking for, for quite some time, as in centuries."

"Are you finished?" A disembodied voice asked. It was emanating from the empty box on the screen.

"Yes, yes, I am." Phillip said, looking a bit confused, as he appeared to not recognize the voice. It did seem to have a bit of a witness-protection-program synthesizer added to it.

"Bravo, my boy. Bravo for the performance the other night. And Bravo for your performance right now." The voice said. "I watched the recording from the other night. Stupendous."

Azramar, looked surprised, bordering on aghast. He muttered, "There were no cameras. There is no recording. Duncan, who is this?"

"Gentlemen, please allow me to introduce the Magnus Gallus, the Supreme Cock himself," Duncan proclaimed. Azramar nearly fell out of his chair. Phillip quickly recovered his composure. For me, I wasn't in the loop. Phillip had mentioned him before, so I knew he was the Top Cock. But at the time, I didn't know the power he wielded.

"Phillip, we will meet most of your demands and do not mention to me again the word, suggestions. We do not govern. We merely counsel. We can suggest the promotion, but we cannot guarantee it, or make it happen in absolute terms or on a particular timetable. Mr. Dong, we extend a gracious hand to you. I hope you will return the favor tenfold for the good of the organization. And, Mr. Dong..."

"Yes sir?" I responded.

"Don't fuck this up," the Magnus Gallus said. Why are people always saying that to me? I thought. "And Phillip, before I go," The MG continued. "We have it on good account that the Undersecretary, your dear professor, will be retiring soon. Thus, we will also be working to line up a promotion for you as well. I suggest you both put in your promotional requisitions. Please, let the Undersecretary tell you this. In other words, you did not hear this from me.

Like me, the professor is up there in years. While he wants to retire, I have no plans to do the same any time soon. I, my friends, am having the time of my life. Don't worry about the professor, we will see he has everything he needs and get him home safe and sound. Enjoy your holiday and, ciao for now." With that the MG signed off.

"Holiday?" I asked.

"Yes," Phillip said. "Because we nailed our performance, we each get a three-day holiday to recuperate at the destination of our choice." Phillips said. He quickly added, "Would you care to join me?

"Yes. Why yes, I would." I said. "Where are we going?"

"Ever been to Mykonos?" Phillip asked.

"No, never," I said.

Cumdumpster then spoke up saying, "I'll call the travel agent and make your reservations. You will still need to be back in DC come Monday evening."

Mycheex quickly added, with a wicked smile on his face, "Don Kee Dong, we need to do your orientation very, very soon. So you'll be coming up to New York in the next couple of weeks to complete your initiation?"

"Yes sir. I look forward to coming to New York and letting you and Mr. Cumdumpster train me in all the HO ways," I said.

"What a great call," Duncan said. "I'm so glad the MG could join us. It just helps us with all the red tape. I wish everyone a good day."

Suddenly Azramar spoke up sounding so polite, "Phillip, would you be so kind as to stay on for a few minutes after everyone says their goodbyes? I just have some logistics I need to cover." I wrote "no" on the shared piece of paper.

Phillip ignored me and said, "Of course."

"Bye."

"Toodeloo."

"Adios," rang out and we were left on the call alone with Azramar who went from pleasant to menacingly hostile in under a millisecond.

"You got away with it this time, but I've got your number. I'm going to get you and your big Dong too!"

Phillip replied in his sassy and endearing way. Endearing when you're not on the receiving end of it, I'm sure. "I certainly hope the MG isn't recording this, making a threat toward HOs number #1 top and bottom power couple could be grounds for dismissal."

"This isn't being recorded!" Azramar, shouted. Though he did look sideways for some unknown reason.

"You're probably right," Phillip said. "It's probably not. Just like there were certainly no cameras in the moon cavern the other night, yet somehow the MG saw it all. Azramar, don't make a war where none exists. I suggest you go take out your anger on five willing bottoms and don't call me in the morning. Now, good day." Phillip hit the disconnect button before Azramar could say another word.

"What about his hard drive and the diamonds?" I asked.

"I'll let him sweat a bit and I'll leave the hard drive here in Prague and tell him later where he can find it. As for the diamonds. They are our insurance policy. I will send him one every six months. That should buy us, 20 years maybe. Perhaps I'll send them more frequently. As far as the hard drive goes, I'll let him know I have a copy and to please treat the information with a little more care in the future. I'll end with, 'don't fuck with me or I'll fuck you over just to keep him on good behavior." It made me hot when he got angry...at someone else.

That night we went to another tucked-away local's-only type restaurant in the neighborhood of our dorm. Phillip said he would often eat here when he was visiting Prague as a student. He said he always thought it was romantic. We clinked our wine glasses together and cheered to our good fortune over a delicious dinner. When we got back to our room, we spooned until my cock grew rock-hard and I fucked him lying sideways on the bed. When I awoke in the morning, I grew a big smile on my face as my hard cock was pressing against the entrance of his tight hole. He moved only slightly, and we were one.

Chapter 25

We checked into our flight to Mykonos that afternoon. Phillip arranged with the Budapest Intercontinental to ship his luggage to our destination. We went to a luggage locker and Phillip deposited the hard drive in one and pocketed the key to mail to Azramar later. We cleared security and made our way to the first-class lounge.

It was just after 8:00 a.m. in DC, so I called my boss, Head Gver, "Dong here," I said.

"Yes, Mr. Dong. To what do I owe this interruption?" he asked.

"You ever hear of Groupon or the entertainment catalog, sir?" I asked.

"No. Why should I have?" he said unimpressed.

"It turns out Mihol is an amazing coupon clipper and bargain shopper. Everything is on the up and up. He uses the Undersecretary's Platinum Am Ex card to get amazing deals. I think we should consider his methods to save the agency money," I said.

"Dong," he interrupted. "He does not save any money. He spends the entirety of the per diem. You went all the way to Budapest to figure that out?" he asked sarcastically.

"Well, I had to see him in action. The hotel alone was in awe of him because he secured such low rates for their top-of-the-line rooms," I said.

"I expect you back in the office tomorrow morning," he commanded.

I started pressing buttons on the phone and making static noises in my throat and mouth. "I can't hear you, sir. You're breaking up. The phone service here is terrible," I said. "If you can hear me, the good news is there is no scandal for the Agency. The Director General will be so pleased with you. Mihol is cleared. Thank you for this opportunity, sir. I'll see you Tuesday morning sir."

"Dong!!!" was the last thing I heard as I hung up.

I was certain there was a meeting with HR in my future. At least they would be "listening."

Epilogue

Our heroes walked hand-in-hand around the island of Mykonos, Greece. They ate freshly caught seafood in romantic restaurants and sat in a hilltop tavern enjoying the backdrop of the sunset in front of storied windmills while drinking champagne.

They got lost while meandering down stone pathways laid out between blue-roofed, whiter-than-white, buildings. They danced in the bars and took a rickety school bus to Super Paradise Beach, and another to Elia Beach. They floated on a two-man dingy in the ocean, lazily entwined in one another's arms and legs, and they swam in their charming hotel's pool. They rented a moped and tooled around the island, Phillip driving and Dong's arms wrapped tightly around him, his hardened cock pressed against Phillip's ass.

They bought gyros from street vendors and licked the dripping white tzatziki sauce off of each other's fingers. But mostly they fucked and they sucked and they licked each other in every which way possible and they always did it to the hilt.

Coming Soon

I hope you have enjoyed reading *The Misadventures of Don Kee Dong and Phillip Mihol: International Men of Mystery.*

This book is the first in my International Men of Mystery series. Watch for my second book in the series, *Assmasters of Asia* in the 2027 season and *Rimming on the Rhine* in 2028.

Gareth Carter

Other forthcoming titles in the series include: *Our Man in Manila*, *The Barebackers of Buenos Aires*, *The Fister of Finland*, *Singapore Sling*, *The Dick from Dakar*, and more.

Follow Gareth Carter (Instagram: @garethcarterauthor or on the web at www.garethcarterauthor.com) for updates.

Acknowledgements

First, I wish to thank the librarians who make up my publishing house for believing in me and this crazy story, and my editor, Eduardo Santiago, who strengthened the story's bones and ensured it could withstand scrutiny, allowing it to land with weight when needed and with laughter when it should.

I am also grateful to the countless librarians who encourage me and stand beside me in the fight against book banners and burners; to my extended family for their support throughout this journey; to my fellow writers for their sage advice; and to the many workshop attendees who endured early drafts of my work.

Most of all, I thank my friends, whose encouragement grew as they witnessed the joy this work brought me while I shared my characters' exploits. I also extend my thanks to Kirkus Reviews and the many media outlets that helped promote this book.

To all of you, I am deeply grateful and in awe of the richness you bring to my life.

www.ingramcontent.com/pod-product-compliance
Lightning Source LLC
Chambersburg PA
CBHW030931060726
47591CB00005B/1757
9781970702002